Pluck Me Sideways

Kelly Violet

Pluck Me Sideways

Published by Pump Up the Violet Publishing, Los Angeles, CA.

Cover design by Crown Designs

Cover content is for illustrative purposes only and any person depicted on the cover is a model.

Library of Congress Control Number: 2025920868

ISBN-13: 978-1-954572-24-9

First Edition

Printed in the U.S.A.

This book goes out to the anyone still looking for your place to bloom.

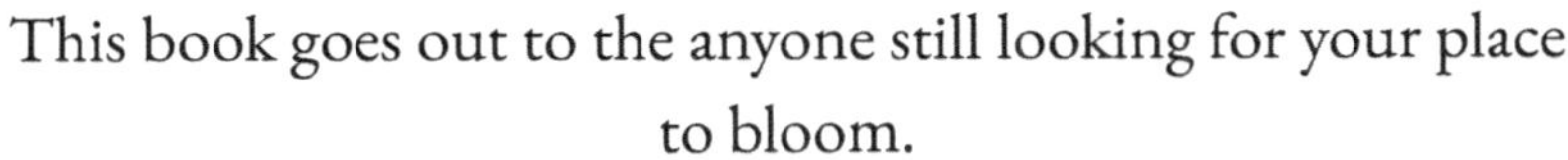

Whatever situation you find yourself in, keep plucking going. You got this!

Chapter One

*B*loom *where you are planted.*

"What a load of crap!" My outburst echoed in the empty space, filled with a level of contempt I couldn't shake no matter how hard I tried. And believe me, I tried damned hard. Now, the gimmicky phrase stamped on the pot of an artificial plant had the nerve to mock me as I stared daggers at it.

Not for the first time I wondered if I should chuck the decorative item in the garbage instead of leaving it in the growing donation pile.

"Ugh, I can't do this right now." Needing a distraction, I lay on my back for a spectacular view of my living room ceiling and pulled up my best friend's number.

Since high school graduation, Candace Matheson and I pursued vastly different paths, but nothing could get in the way of our decade-long friendship. And that knowledge alone had me calling her up to vent my frustrations for the nth time.

The moment the call connected I went in. "Nowhere on my bingo card did it say I'd be quitting my job and uprooting my life."

"Zinn, calm down and stop being so damn extra. You're twenty-five going on twenty-six. Starting over right now won't be the end of the world." Candace chuckled.

"Go ahead and laugh at my pain then." This heavy mass weighing on my chest still hadn't left. "So why does it feel like it is, though? This is not at all what I had planned."

"Yeah, I know."

"Institutional bullshit politics."

"Get it all off your chest," Candace encouraged half-heartedly, but her words were exactly the reason I called her and not someone else. No matter how many times I vented, she gave me the space, and I've done the same for her.

It was the hallmark of our friendship, especially now that we didn't share the same zip code. *At least that will change pretty damn soon.*

"I can't believe this school. As much work and effort as I put into this place, you'd think they would reward me with some type of leadership opportunity, even a minor one. Hell, I was one of the few actually vying for more responsibility."

"I know. And your next employer will certainly value you more."

"Let's hope." Five years down the drain. While only three of those years were as a full-time employee, I worked my ass off to provide exceptional service. And don't even get me started on being a team player. Hell, if there was an entry in the dictionary, my smiling face should've been printed right next to it.

"Not one leadership opportunity at this place. They tapped the same damned mediocre people each time. Why not me, huh?" I pitched in without being asked, going above and beyond more than any of my other colleagues. But no matter how much I did or gave, it never seemed like enough.

"That place doesn't deserve you, Zinn. You're meant for bigger and better things."

"From your lips to God's ears, Candy." What got my goat the most was the fact that nothing changed after pressing send on my resignation email. I'd spent a weekend drowning my sorrows in wine and chocolate before giving up the ghost. Then, I damn near chipped my nails typing up cover letters and applying to half a dozen jobs across the country.

By the end of that same week—when the rash urge hadn't left or dissipated even a little—I clicked send on the email waiting in my drafts folder.

At the time, I remembered the seconds passing at a slow crawl even while the clock never stopped ticking. But no one busted into my cubicle, demanding to know what the hell I was thinking. My passive aggressive boss never came around to try to dissuade me from quitting. There was no counteroffer put on the proverbial table for me to consider.

Not a damn thing had changed except the fact that I had to come to grips and accept that working at my alma mater was doing nothing for me. And I was no longer willing to deal with the bullshit, getting passed over for project leadership, and being pushed to the sidelines. Not when I had just as much, if not more, motivation than my colleagues.

Ugh, my thoughts were spiraling again which got me nowhere fast but stuck in a cycle of bitterness, and I was done with that mess. Done with a job that hardly valued what I brought to the table. I needed to be at a place where I could learn and grow. Somewhere that allowed my strengths and creativity to shine through instead of stunting and burying them.

"You have every right to feel the way you do, Zinn, but don't let those feelings control you. There are new opportunities on the horizon. Don't forget that."

Candace's voice broke through the thick fog of grudgery I was stewing in. "I know. And we'll be back in the same zip code, too. Well, sometimes."

"I know. I'm super excited about that. I miss my best friend."

"Me too, girl. But you're living your best life traveling the world. When are you home next?" Intent on switching gears, I asked about her schedule. There was no telling how often we'd get to hang out even though I was moving back to Dallas soon.

"I'm home now, but I'll be in Europe by the time your flight lands." She was always on the go, and I envied that about her. Since we were little, Candace talked about seeing the world. Now, she gets to do it one flight at a time. "If anything comes up when you get back don't hesitate to call my brother."

"Um, thanks but you know I hate to be a bother. And I'm sure the last thing Campbell wants to do is have me dumping a problem on him."

"Zinn, you know that's the furthest thing from the truth. You're family. And Camp would lend a hand in a hot minute when it comes to you." Unsure if she meant that how it sounded, I decided not to get my hopes up.

"Yeah, okay," I said to brush off her comments. But the sudden shift to talking about her twin brother got me all kinds of flustered.

Unlike my best friend, Campbell Matheson had a will and a way about him that worked my last nerve. Maybe it was because I low-key fell in love with him at fourteen years old, and those feelings hadn't magically evaporated now that I'm older and smarter.

"Speaking of your family, how is everyone?" I wasn't just trying to get the tea on her brother with my question. At least that was the lie I told myself.

"My parents are great. You know I got the travel bug from them, and they are currently touring around Ireland and

Scotland. If our schedules align just right, I might be able to see them on one leg of my trip."

"Hopefully it works out."

"Right? And Camp is Camp. He's fine." *Damn straight he is!* I rolled my eyes at the runaway thought. There was zero time to fantasize about my best friend's twin brother. A guy who loved to tease me and say anything to get under my skin. Nothing downright hurtful or menacing, mind you, since it didn't stop me from harboring a ridiculous crush. Still, I knew better.

"Well, I'll let you get back to whatever you were doing, Candy. And I should stop procrastinating and pack some shit." I pushed up from my position on the floor and took in all of the big and small tasks I had yet to finish.

"Okay. Send me updates on everything. I may only be able to reply intermittently, but you know I'm here for whatever you need."

"Thanks! Talk to you soon."

"Bye, Zinn."

In the quiet of the room, my mind wandered for a bit. Thoughts of that social life I promised myself I would seek out in Santa Barbara evaporated before I even got a chance to try things out. The biggest regret was not attending one of the meetings of the Plucking Ladies Garden Club. I had high hopes of connecting with women and building a solid friend group. Outside of Candace and a few people I kept in contact with, my circle was tight knit.

"Maybe I can send a message to Violet to see if there's a chapter or similar type of group near Dallas," I thought out loud. Promising myself I would reach out to ask, I got back to work packing up the remainder of my life in California.

Ten days later I was on a plane heading to Dallas. Since my parents had me in their early forties, they were already retired and moved to Michigan to be closer to my father's relatives. The family I had left in Dallas I wasn't particularly close to, so I was essentially moving back on my own. There was Candace and her family, but they were hardly ever in Texas. Except Campbell.

The moment the wheels touched down at DFW, I switched off airplane mode and waited for my phone signal. I couldn't wait to get to my new apartment and unpack the boxes I managed to send ahead of time.

My phone vibrated and pinged with various messages. Seeing the voicemail icon pop up on the screen, I decided to listen to it before checking anything else. What I heard chilled my bones. Calling back, my heart thumped hard and heavy in my chest as I waited for the call to connect.

Seconds felt like hours until someone picked up. "Hi, this is Zinnia Whitfield, I received a message in regard to the apartment I plan to move into today."

"Yes, Ms. Whitfield, we've been trying to reach you all day." I rolled my eyes at the blatant lie since I haven't been unreachable all day, just for the past three hours while I've been in the air.

"I'm confused about what the issue is as I've paid the first, last, and deposit. There are boxes outside my door waiting for me which your office said wouldn't be a problem. I just need to pick up the key before six p.m. today, correct?"

"Ms. Whitfield, I'm sorry to tell you this, but the apartment you secured is no longer available. We had a glitch in our system."

"Excuse me?" My brain couldn't compute what the apartment complex manager said.

"We no longer have a vacant apartment for you to move into. I'm sorry."

"Are you telling me I no longer have a place to live?!" My outburst came at the same moment the plane arrived at the gate, the overhead lights coming on like an ill-timed spotlight. The heat of several pairs of eyes on me kept my meltdown at bay. At least until I got off the aircraft then who knew what waited for me.

My mind raced after ending the call. The manager assured me that she would move my belongings into the office until I was able to retrieve them. Every last penny of my funds would be returned at that time as well. *Small favors.*

Pushed forward and off the plane by the wave of impatient travelers, I found myself with my backpack and carry-on bag sitting at a random gate. I would need to grab my other luggage from baggage claim before too long. But then what?

Candace was already in Europe. I wouldn't bother my parents with this until I had a solution. And there was no one in my extended family I dared to call.

You have to call him, a voice in my head whispered. I tried to shrug the idea away, but my brain wouldn't let me. Or my common sense. Campbell Matheson was my last resort. In all honesty, he was my one and only option.

Sucking in a long breath, my hands shook as I pulled up his number. The call connected almost immediately.

"Camp, I-I need your help."

"Where are you?"

"Stranded at the airport."

"You're finally home?"

"Yes?" His breathless question had butterflies swirling in my belly.

"I'm on my way." He clicked off before I could stutter out a thank you. Now that I knew Campbell was on his way, I breathed a little easier since getting the fucked-up news about my apartment. I had so much shit to do before anything would be okay.

Losing my new home because of a computer glitch or someone's ineptitude, more like, was also not on my bingo card for the year. This bullshit was on another fucking level.

It felt like I was drowning in a sea of shitty decisions, and the one person I could count on right now was the person I wanted to see the least.

We'd known each other long enough that I expected him to treat me as an extension of his twin sister. The very last thing I wanted from him. But that wasn't going to change, and I had to come to grips with that fact. Close the door to imagining anything else.

But he was coming for me, and I had to muster up some way to guard my heart when I laid eyes on him for the first time in over seven years.

It wasn't gonna be easy. Hell, it was gonna be damn near impossible. But there was literally no other choice.

Pluck my life!

Chapter Two

I raced to the airport like my future depended on it, and maybe it did. My girl had finally come home. She said she needed me, and there wasn't a damned thing to keep me from getting to her.

The news of her return hadn't been a complete surprise to me since I counted on my sister to keep me updated on anything and everything to do with her best friend. Although we had all hung out together since middle school, I'd kept myself pretty much to the periphery of their friendship. Playing the big brother role to a T, even though I was only a few minutes older than Candace, that meant I stayed in protective mode almost all the time. Which had quickly extended to Zinnia, too.

And all throughout high school, nothing stopped me from teasing the beauty every chance I could. The immature behavior kept my interest in her somewhat at bay. Feelings I'd realized were more desire than friendship. More possessive than protective. Before I knew what hit me, graduation rolled around and by the end of that summer, she was gone.

My heart dropped at the almost eight-year-old memory. From all that I gleaned from my sister's updates, Zinn's life in California had been going well enough until recently. Then, her situation at work got progressively worse as my girl decided to look for other opportunities.

Selfishly, I wanted her to find her way back home. Back to me. And someone above looked out for me because I got my wish. All I had to do was make it count.

Even when we were younger, I knew how important Zinnia was in my life. Although I'd kept my distance, I had my reasons. Reasons that seemed all but moot now.

Twenty-five minutes after jumping in my truck, I arrived at the airport. Only slightly surprised that a row of police cruisers wasn't behind me with the way I disregarded every single traffic law to get here. But that was Texas for you. I hadn't been the only one doing crazy shit on the way here.

I'd been in such a hurry to get to the airport that I missed out on asking follow-up questions like which airline. So, I kept my eyes peeled as I slowed the car and looked for any sign of my girl at Arrivals.

Sweat beaded on my brow as the seconds ticked by. The inside of my car was too quiet. I'd been too focused on my mission to get to her that everything else faded to the background.

"Where are you, Zinn?" Traffic came to a pause which gave me an opportunity to glance at my phone, hoping that she'd sent me a message with some details. And my prayers were answered with a text that included her airline and current location.

Once the cars ahead of me started moving again, I talked myself down. Navigating airport traffic always felt like a special level of hell, but I couldn't let impatient assholes and shit drivers get to me. Not today.

I tapped my fingers on the steering wheel while inching forward, waiting for that precious moment when I laid eyes on my dream girl. I was so on edge that it felt like I waited another eight years for her return in the last several minutes.

No one would ever call me a saint, especially in the past decade, but I'd known Zinnia would be my endgame. All I had to do was convince her that we belonged together. And I knew damn well it wouldn't be easy. My girl had a stubborn streak a mile long and a mouth that could make grown men weep. But those were the traits I appreciated most about her when we were younger. She wasn't one to hold her tongue when it came to me and my antics, and I looked forward to learning how my girl had changed over the years and in what ways she remained exactly how I remember her.

I geared myself up for a different type of education. One I was ready and willing to dive into.

The sea of cars parted as I finally approached Zinnia's location. Not more than ten seconds passed before I spotted her. A sight for sore eyes.

Her call had come as a complete shock. Whether I was her first option or last resort mattered little to me as I drank in her petite and curvy form.

Impatient like never before, the truck came to an abrupt halt next to where she stood on the curb. Jumping out of the driver's side, I was in front of her in less than thirty seconds. *Hell, I don't think she's even had time to register my arrival.* But nothing short of a natural disaster would've kept me away. *And maybe not even that,* I thought to myself.

Our gazes connected, and everything stopped like one of those freeze-frame scenes. Her big, brown eyes widened, and I got lost in them. For some unknown reason, the urge to open my arms wide slammed into me, so I did. Her reaction seemed almost instant, she moved so fast. And dammit if I didn't love the feeling of her in my arms. Every muscle in my body vibrated from the unscripted embrace.

"You okay, Zinn?"

"Not really. But thank you for picking up my call and coming to get me."

"No thanks necessary." *There's nothing I wouldn't do for you.*

Sadly, our hug ended as she pushed away from me, and I dropped my arms and took a small step back to give her space.

"Let's get your luggage in the truck and then you can tell me what's going on."

"Okay." Her voice was soft. Too small for as much space as she'd taken up in my head. Deep down I knew it was all temporary, this cloud of despair hanging over her head right now. When she went to reach for the handles of her luggage, I stopped her.

"Just get in the truck, Zinn. I got this." Shoulders slumped, the fight had all but left her, which wasn't like my girl at all. Whatever worries plagued her, I'd do everything in my power to make them disappear.

Now that she was back, I wanted to keep her here. With me.

Opening the passenger-side door, I waited until she got settled in the seat before closing the door and then I placed her luggage in the bed of my truck. It seemed like she had too few items to be moving back home for good, but now wasn't the time to ask. There were other pressing matters like what had her calling me out of the blue.

Two minutes later, I hopped back into the driver's seat and pulled away from the curb. It would take us several minutes to leave the airport and get on the highway. Hopefully, I'd have a better sense of the situation by that time.

"Talk to me, Zinn. What's going on?"

"I'm basically homeless all because of a supposed computer glitch. But if you ask me, someone doesn't know how to do their goddamn job," she seethed.

"Rewind for a second. You lost your apartment?"

"I didn't lose anything. They did. And don't ask me how, it wouldn't make sense even if I tried to explain it to you. Fuck, I don't understand it myself."

"Okay, what can I do?" The gears in my brain started shifting, wanting to figure out a way to fix everything for her.

"Can you take me to the apartment complex? I mailed several boxes ahead, and the manager said she'd keep them in the office until I retrieved them. They also better have a check waiting for me."

"Where am I heading? We'll figure out the rest after that." Zinnia rattled off the address of the apartment complex. I knew the area since it was a few miles from where my twin sister lived.

I drove in relative silence as my little spitfire sat mere inches away from me, vibrating with a mix of anger and worry. What she hadn't realized yet was there was nothing I wouldn't do for her. I'd make damned sure her worries faded to nothing before the end of the day.

Forty minutes later, we arrived at the apartment complex. At just before five o'clock on a weekday, the neighborhood appeared almost calm and pristine. And then there was Zinnia whose energy was anything but tranquil. She tapped her left foot against the floorboard, and I didn't notice the fidgeting until I stopped and turned off the engine.

"Are you ready?" I turned my head to ask, my breath stalling at her beauty. Her long eyelashes fluttered, eyes closing as she took a moment to breathe slowly. Once her pretty brown gaze met mine again, I knew she'd be okay even if Zinn had her doubts.

"Yes, let's get this over with. The faster we get out of here, the quicker I can find a hotel for the next few nights."

"There's not a chance in hell you're staying at a hotel, Zinn."

"Campbell..." Whatever expression she saw on my face stopped the rest of the sentence from leaving her mouth.

"You're not alone." I held her gaze too long, unwilling to break our stare-down, but my point needed to be made. Still, I broke the tension by adding, "And my place has plenty of room. You can stay as long as you need. It's not a problem. Not even a little bit." *Plus, if I have my way, you won't find a reason to leave anytime soon.*

The possessive bastard in me was alive and well; I'd come to find out. But only when it came to Zinnia.

"I won't fight you on this." She hadn't said *yet*, but that didn't stop me from hearing it all the same. "Let's go to the manager's office and get my boxes. I'll feel better once I have all of my stuff."

"I'm sure you will."

We hopped out of the truck, my long strides had me reaching her on the sidewalk in no time. I matched her steps as we marched toward a sign directing us to the office.

My gaze wandered during the short walk. I noted the manicured grounds and the exterior of the apartment complex. From the outside, things appeared to be maintained and cared for on the property, but maybe that was all just a well-designed facade for unsuspecting future residents like my girl.

We'd find out soon enough, I reckoned.

Zinnia was right on one thing, though. The sooner we picked up her stuff, the faster I could get her home which was my ultimate end goal.

After getting my day started, I had a pretty good idea of how most of it would play out. I wasn't exactly in rinse and repeat mode, but some days felt damn close to that. In an instant, Zinnia's call for help pushed the mundane away and like hell would I ever complain. Somehow, I'd hit the jackpot without buying a single lottery ticket. It almost felt like the universe knew how desperate I was to see her again and finally set my plans in motion. Lay claim to my twin sister's best friend once and for all. Something I was too young, arrogant, and immature to do back in high school.

With the office door in front of us, I reached down to grasp her hand, giving it a squeeze in case she needed reassurance. Instead of dropping or shrugging the gesture off, she held firm, and I wanted to pump my other fist in the air.

Opening the door, she entered the space while I stayed close behind her.

"Hello. Can I help you folks with something?" A well-dressed woman in her early thirties, if I had to guess, stood up from behind a desk placed in the center of the large, open workspace.

"I sure hope so," Zinn started with a hint of honey in her tone, which had my dick twitching. Now was not the time for that. Standing by her side, I let her handle the issue, paying as much attention as possible in case she needed me to step in. Our hands remained locked while Zinnia spoke with the apologetic manager as if the connection with me grounded her somehow.

Down boy, I tried keeping myself in check. For the time being at least. Once I got her home and settled, though, all bets were off.

Surely, I had my work cut out for me. Good thing I was a man who wasn't afraid of a hard day's work.

I hope you're ready for me, Zinn, because I'm not letting you go this time.

Chapter Three

Anxiety mixed with rage, simmering in the pit of my stomach as I listened to the apartment complex manager rattle off one excuse after another. Yet and still, nothing she said magically got me a new set of keys and an apartment to move into.

"Again, we're sorry for the mix-up and inconvenience. If any apartment should become available in the next month or so, you'll be the first person I call." She handed me a check for the online payments I made not more than a week prior. *At least I'd have these funds back in my account in a couple days.* "Your boxes are by the door." Both Campbell and I turned to look over our shoulders, seeing the five large boxes where she indicated.

"Thank you for your time." *And for ruining my day.*

Going to turn, my brain zoomed in on the fact that mine and Campbell's hands were still interlocked. I quickly disengaged, wondering what the hell was wrong with me. Gripping his hand like it was a lifeline or something. I shook my head.

Bending down, I lifted one of the boxes while Campbell grabbed two. The manager hustled over to hold the door open for us.

"I'll be right back to get the last two," he said as we made our way back to his truck. In minutes, we had the three boxes loaded alongside my luggage on the bed of his truck, and then he jogged back to get the last two. The infuriating man had stopped me with a hard look when I offered to go back to the office with him. I rolled my eyes the moment his back turned and leaned against his tailgate, waiting for his return.

What the hell am I supposed to do now? With my new job starting in two weeks' time, I still had to go in to complete the final paperwork, make sure the rest of my belongings currently on a truck from California got delivered somewhere, and find a new place to live. Easy peasy, right?

I also had to somehow deal with the guy striding towards me carrying two big-ass boxes as if they weighed next to nothing. He'd offered me a place to stay without missing a beat, and I'd yet to wrap my head around any of it. Not me calling him out of the blue and him dropping everything to scoop me up from the airport. Especially not the same guy who's been my longest crush and biggest headache. I wanted to scream at how easily he's stirred up my feelings in several different ways, and it's only been a damned hour. *What the hell am I supposed to do once we get to his place, and I'm stuck there?* With the current housing market, I counted myself lucky that I'd found the apartment when I did. And that all managed to blow up in my face in spectacular fashion.

Switching gears, I watched Campbell's approach and got my fill of him. The muscles and veins of his bare forearms twitched as he moved. Since our teens, he'd been built like a farm boy. Tall and wide, his physique was nice and strong from all the summers and weekends spent working construction and landscaping jobs. He'd been a hot guy back in high school, but damn it all if he hadn't grown into one fine-ass specimen. A bona fide snack. And my thirsty behind suddenly became peckish.

Pluck it all, I need to think about something else. Anything else. Like the dismal state of my life right now. Not even a full two hours since my plane landed, and things had gone straight to hell. My one saving grace was that I wouldn't be out on the street. Not when a knight in a flannel shirt driving a shiny truck came to my rescue.

It seemed like my only option was staying with a guy I hadn't seen in person since high school graduation. It didn't matter that we grew up together. Or that I knew things about him that I probably shouldn't. His sister usually became a fountain of information when she wanted to be. And when the topic of her family inevitably came up in our occasional chats, I never had the heart to stop her word vomit once she landed on the goings-on of Campbell.

The years and distance apart didn't stop the man from living rent-free in my heart even though I knew better. At least that's what I lied and told myself time and time again. I never could've imagined my first official day back ending up quite like this. *But here we are.*

With the truck bed loaded up with the last remaining boxes, we got back on the road in no time at all. Now that one thing had been taken care of, my mind raced with several more worries. Like how the hell would I find a place to live before my new job started in two weeks?

I thought I'd given myself some buffer between the move and my start. Clearly, I'd been delusional.

"Let's grab food on the way home," Camp said, his voice slicing through the silence and my circular train of thoughts.

"Um, okay."

"Anything you might be in the mood for, Zinn?"

You, the sex-starved part of my brain supplied without my permission. Thankfully, nothing embarrassing popped out of my mouth.

"You choose. I don't know what's good around here anymore."

Stopped at a light, I glanced at him and our gazes clashed. The expression on his handsome face that seemed filled with a gentle understanding put me in a chokehold. I broke eye contact right as the light turned green and traffic started moving again.

I needed to get a grip quickly. Or else this temporary situation had disaster written all over it. To make this work, I had better get us back to our usual M.O. Although his sister was my bestie, which meant I saw him way too often growing up, the two of us ran hot and cold with each other.

Not used to this empathetic and mature version of my long-time nemesis and hidden crush, my emotions were all over the place. Hell, I was pretty sure my heart couldn't take much more of his unexpected warmth.

Making a turn, he maneuvered into the drive-thru lane of a Mexican restaurant. Once we placed our orders and inched our way towards the next window, I shifted in the passenger seat to face him.

"I promise not to overstay my welcome, Camp. I'll get out of your hair as soon as possible. Maybe I can stay at Candy's place for a few days since she's never home."

"No."

I lifted my eyebrows in shock. *Say what now?* My brain stuttered for a second. "Whaddya mean 'no'?" I finally forced the question out.

He clenched his jaw. Mesmerized, I watched as his muscles ticked a few times in a row. His long and measured intake of breath said everything and nothing. *What the hell crawled up his ass and died?*

Ready to fix my mouth to say something, he spoke first. "You don't have to be so considerate, Zinn. I have plenty of room, and you're welcome to stay as long as you need." He eased up on the brakes to inch forward more and then turned to gaze at me. "I mean that, okay. I know that you're starting your new job in a couple weeks. If finding a place to stay will take up too much time, then don't for now."

It was our turn to pull up to the payment window, which Campbell took care of. I made sure to thank him but kept my mouth shut about paying for my own food. Something told me the offer wouldn't go over well with the way his jaw still twitched off and on as I watched him out of the corner of my eye.

With the bag containing our dinner on my lap, we got back on the road. The silence became even louder than before. I couldn't explain how the vibes had shifted, but there was a different air in the car.

I stifled a sigh, keeping my attention on the passing scenery. Curiosity got the best of me as we entered a quiet neighborhood, and I tried to imagine what I'd find at Camp's place. A bachelor pad or something more.

A few minutes passed before he pulled into the driveway of a one-story house situated on a corner lot.

Several homes on the street had mature trees, including his. So far, I was itching to hop out of the truck and nose around. Camp's home held most of my interest, but I also wanted to wander around his neighborhood to my heart's content.

Maybe it would give me some insight into the guy next to me since I only really had a clear impression of him as a boy. Not this grown-up version of the man who still, even to this day, popped up in my dreams from time to time.

Maybe that's why my first instinct was to call him even though I had no business doing so. Too late to regret it now, I reached for the door only to realize in my daze, Camp had already gotten out and came around to open it for me. Helping me down, Campbell grabbed the food bag on my lap and took my hand.

My heart stupidly skipped at the unexpected gesture. Telling myself to calm the hell down, I shook off the comforting touch as soon as my feet met the asphalt of his driveway. "Thanks," I managed to blurt.

"How about I give you a quick tour first and then we can eat?"

"Okay." Dealing with my luggage and those boxes held little appeal at the moment, so I jumped on his offer of a temporary distraction like some sort of salvation.

My life was a mess and a half right now, and I knew my situation wouldn't be fixed overnight, but at least I could ignore reality a smidge longer.

The moment I stepped over the threshold and entered his home, I was screwed.

Because when the time came for me to leave, I had a feeling it would break my heart.

Chapter Four

I carried our food while unlocking my front door and holding it open for Zinnia. Her first impression of my home mattered more than just a little. I needed her to like my place enough to not want to start looking for one of her own immediately.

Call me a selfish and possessive bastard, but I didn't care. Now that she was back and standing next to me, I couldn't let her go without a serious fight.

Hearing her already talk about leaving before even getting settled at my place for the night had my jaw clenching. The refusal had been automatic. The innate brute inside of me uttered 'no' without regret even as Zinnia's neck snapped around to stare at me like I was some crazy person.

Obviously, we both changed over the years. Hell, I grew up in a lot of ways after graduating high school and trying to figure out what came next. There had been more than a few hits and misses before landing on my calling. I imagined Zinnia had her own growing pains going to college and finding her way in a new state.

But no matter the time or distance apart, I knew she was meant to be mine. Just like I knew when we were younger. The difference now was that I had concrete things to offer.

"Campbell, your home…" Zinnia stood there frozen as I held the door open. Something got her moving a few seconds later, and I closed the front door while watching her take in the space.

I was proud of my home. It had been the third property I flipped with the intention of selling, but my plans shifted partway through completely gutting the place, and I hadn't looked back. I liked having a home base between projects, and it gave me a sense of peace.

Once Zinnia spent some time here I hoped she felt the same.

"So, what do you think?"

She spun around, a big smile stretching her sexy lips. "Your place is amazing, Camp. It really is."

"Thanks. That means a lot." She didn't even know. Hopefully soon, she would. "Let's eat. Follow me to the kitchen. Did you wanna heat up anything?"

"Nah, I think I'm good," she answered distractedly. I wanted to stop and watch her discover every nook and corner but forced myself to move forward. Even if I refused to voice all of my thoughts out loud, I promised to slow down. We had plenty of time to relearn each other, especially the details my twin sister wasn't privy to or neglected to mention.

Placing the bag on the countertop, we descended on our containers wordlessly. I saw a visible drop to Zinnia's shoulders, hoping that some of her stress evaporated now that she was safe and sound with me. In my home.

Fuck, I had a mind to scoop her over my shoulder and march us to my bedroom. Lay claim to her body and heart in all the ways I imagined doing over the years. She wouldn't know what hit her. And if I had my way, neither of us would come up for air for days.

Dick semi-hard and pushing uncomfortably against my boxer briefs, I put a pin in those caveman thoughts.

I was more than ready to prove that she belonged here with me, but Zinnia's mind was likely preoccupied with other things. Namely her living situation.

I scarfed down my dinner in minutes while she ate much slower. Almost as if she savored every bite. I stood there quietly watching her, listening to the soft murmurs of enjoyment she made. That was one trait that hadn't changed about her. Zinnia's outward enjoyment of things. Or the times her face couldn't hide her emotions or thoughts. What had changed was how much I missed and now craved her sounds. I wanted to hear and learn each moan and sigh coming from her and what caused them. Hell, I wanted to be the cause for every good sound and the fixer to every bad one.

"Want the tour and then we can go grab your stuff from the truck?"

"Sure. Lead the way, Camp."

She went back and forth between the given and shortened versions of my name, and it didn't take a rocket scientist to figure out which one my dick preferred hearing.

"Actually, this was the third house I brought to flip. Early on in the process, I realized I wouldn't be able to part with it."

"Candy mentioned you flip houses now. Do you enjoy it?"

"I do. I get to work with my hands. Plus, there's nothing like choosing the next project to work on."

"That sounds right up your alley."

I showed off the living room, kitchen, and dining area then moved us to one of my favorite spaces in the house. Even though I hadn't figured out what to do with the flex room, it had tons of potential. Looking at Zinnia, maybe there was another reason my immediate need to fill the space never materialized. Again, patience was a virtue.

Next, I took her to the three bedrooms, pointing out that one had become a makeshift office space that she was free to use anytime. Next, I showed her my bedroom with its California king, dark furniture, and en-suite bathroom. Through it all, she oohed and aahed at all the appropriate times, sending some serious signals to my two heads.

Lastly, our final stop on the tour was the room that had already become hers in my mind.

"It's perfect, Camp."

"There's space in the closet for your stuff. And you'll have the bathroom right across the hall all to yourself."

"I, um, can't thank you enough for letting me crash at your place temporarily."

"Really, it's not a problem. I told you there's more than enough space for you here. Make yourself at home, and don't feel like you have to rush finding a place."

She nodded, finally seeing and hearing the truth in my words. At least I hoped that was the case. Only time would tell, though.

"I'll head out and start bringing your luggage and boxes in." I pointed a thumb over my shoulder as my feet backed up, thinking I'd give her a bit of space.

"I'll come with you."

"Alright." There was no point in denying her. Plus, the task of bringing her things in would go quicker with the two of us.

On the way back through the house, I pointed out the backyard. Being Fall, the sun had already set as we ate and then took the short tour. I didn't have much out there besides a grill and some lawn chairs for the occasional times I sat outside.

"Mi casa es su casa," I said one last time to get my point across. "You're free to use any and everything here. Make yourself at home, Zinn."

"Okay, thanks." This softer, shy version of her voice did odd things to me. Another vision of tossing her over my shoulder came to mind. The possessive side of me kept getting louder in my head, throwing around words like *mine* and *forever*.

I was on hyperdrive and needed to slow the hell down. This would only work if Zinnia stayed. I had to focus on her comfort, first and foremost before jumping head-first into the feelings I harbored and then making sure to take her with me.

In no time at all, we brought her belongings inside the house in three trips.

Making sure she had what she needed between the room and the hallway bathroom, I left her alone to get settled and start the process of unpacking. The urge to hover and observe rode me hard, but I resisted. Barely. Just hearing her moving around in my home had to be enough for now.

On edge and not the least bit tired, I grabbed a beer from the fridge and took it to the living room. Maybe watching TV would quiet the noise rattling around in my head and keep me from becoming Zinnia's shadow.

I spent several minutes toggling between streaming services before selecting a superhero movie. I'd seen it once in theaters when it first released, but it had been a couple years. Hitting the play button, I let the story pull me in. Or at least tried my damnedest too. But with the soft sounds coming from the bedroom down the hall, my attention was shot to hell.

Not accustomed to the sound of another person in my home, it wasn't unwelcome in the slightest, but it would take some getting used to.

Halfway through the movie that no longer held any sort of appeal, I hit pause on the remote and stood up to throw away my empty bottle and contemplated grabbing another one.

The moment of quiet stretched until I heard a door opening and closing. The sound of light footsteps reached my ears somehow. Everything stalled around me as soon as she turned the corner and came into view. For some inexplicable reason I had to remember how to breathe.

Zinnia had changed clothes. She appeared soft, sweet, and incredibly comfy in what I could only describe as baggy-style loungewear but dammit if her look didn't make me ache as if she came out wearing the slinkiest lingerie.

Mouth dry, I licked my lips for something to do other than swallow my tongue. "What's up?"

"Not much. Thought I would come out and join you?"

"Just going to grab another beer. You want one?"

"Why not. After today's nonsense, I think I deserve one."

"You do," I agreed. "Feel free to start the movie over or find something else to watch."

"You sure?" She tiptoed toward the sectional sofa, eyes on the screen to see what I had on."

"It's fine. I wasn't that invested to begin with."

"Okay." It seemed like we'd settled into this sort of unspoken truce, the verbal sparring of our youth over the dumbest stuff far behind us. I wasn't mad at the current situation even if I loved how beautiful Zinnia looked when she gave me shit.

After grabbing our beers, I slowed my steps on the way back to the living room so that I could observe her. It took her no time at all to get comfortable on the sofa, legs tucked underneath her as she commandeered one of the lounge cushions on the sectional. She looked good there. Like she belonged and already became a permanent fixture.

Before she caught me staring like some creep, I forced myself to move forward.

Discarding my work boots by the door after the last trip from the truck, I walked around the house in my socks. Even though my size made me hard to miss, I could be light on my feet when I wanted to be.

So, when I extended my arm to pass a beer to Zinnia and touched the cold bottle to her cheek, she startled.

"I couldn't resist."

She arched a perfectly manicured eyebrow at the same time glaring at me. "I just bet you couldn't."

I could see in her eyes that she wanted to snatch the bottle out of my hand and maybe chuck the damn thing at my head but thought better of it. Holding back a laugh, I sat in the middle of the sofa, sitting as close to her as I dared.

"What did you choose?"

"There's a buddy comedy I didn't get to watch in theaters last year." She took a sip of the beer.

"Let's watch it," I told her, and she hit the play button.

The opening scene started, and I realized my focus was even more shot to hell than before. Having her within touching distance played havoc on my self-control.

I lifted the new beer bottle to my lips for something to do. Zinnia's soft, throaty laugh seconds later almost had the liquid going down the wrong pipe. My dick strained even as that poorly timed gulp sent me into a coughing fit.

"Camp, are you okay?" A long moment passed before I could answer her. By then, she'd already paused the movie and scooted closer to me.

Fuck, how can her response be the best and worst thing at the same damned time?

When the feeling of her hand rubbing my back registered, it about did me in. Embarrassment sliced through me even as my dick jerked at the attention. Dammit, I had lost my ever-loving mind, and I was almost positive it wasn't coming back anytime soon.

"Give me one second, and I'll grab some water." With the need to cough finally subsiding, I stopped her right before she untangled herself and got up from the couch.

"I'm good, Zinn." My throat felt scratchy as I scraped the words together, hoping they sounded believable.

"You sure?" But her expression said it all. As long as I'd known her, every thought was plain to see. She couldn't play poker worth a damn because her face hid nothing. That was one of the main reasons I enjoyed teasing her so much in our teens.

But now, her face showed her worry and called me a dumbass in ten different kinda ways. My current predicament was laughable. At least my dick stopped causing me trouble through the coughing fit.

"Really I'm good," I assured her. Zinnia's dark brown gaze looking me over sent a sharp pang to my chest. First time seeing her face to face in years and I went from her hero to a zero in a matter of hours.

I wanted to shake my head at the ridiculousness of it all. Pretty much back to normal, I sat there for another moment before getting up and going to the kitchen. Grabbing two glasses, I got both of us water and tried for casual while heading back to the living room and Zinn.

Fuck! How am I making a complete ass of myself in my own home? No answer came to me. My inner voice was suspiciously quiet at the moment.

"Here you go."

Zinnia accepted the glass with a question in her eyes that, thankfully, she decided not to voice this time. I reclaimed the same spot, unable to distance myself even with the embarrassment still lingering in the air. "Let's finish the movie."

"Mm," she agreed.

In order to gain the upper hand again and not look completely inept in front of Zinnia, I had my work cut out for me. Luckily, I knew exactly how to put in overtime to get the job done. And exceed expectations. Especially the ones I set myself.

My life consisted of creating timelines and hitting milestones, sometimes ahead of schedule whenever possible.

So, as the movie played in the background of my thoughts, a new plan formed. *Get the girl of my dreams to finally return my feelings at all costs*. No exception.

Chapter Five

The first week at Camp's place sped by. We fell into this hazy state of normal domesticity that should've alarmed me. It was just too damned easy.

Nothing weird or exciting happened. Our routines melded together, seemingly matching up with no effort at all. Since he was apparently between projects, Camp stuck close to home, searching current listings and doing whatever else one did when they considered their next investment property to flip.

Anytime we crossed paths in the morning or afternoon, he appeared busy. Meanwhile, I did my best impression of a bum most days, lounging around and biding my time until my new job started.

With more common sense than money at the moment, it became my mission to stick close to Camp's home. Plus, the last of my things were set to arrive from California in a matter of days. My voice was damn near hoarse after all of the calls I made explaining the situation. To my surprise, no one gave me too much trouble about updating the previously scheduled delivery so that my car arrived at Camp's address instead of the sketchy apartment complex.

I could breathe a lot easier, laying that particular worry to bed.

Although I wasn't being my most productive self, I managed to unpack my luggage and boxes, essentially moving into my best friend's brother's house. Every time the thought came to me, my brain broke a little more.

This was not at all how I'd envisioned my homecoming. At the very least, I expected to spend time with Candy to get reacclimated and prepare myself to see Campbell again at some point down the line. But alas, my luck had dried up on that score. Now, I found myself under his roof with few options at my disposal. At least this way, I could start the new job, save up those first few paychecks, and consider my finances at a later date.

Thinking about doing anything sooner than two months from now gave me a stress headache and had my anxiety at an all-time high. Still, feeling utterly useless wasn't in my nature either so I decided to do what I could around the house, namely cooking.

My culinary skills weren't fancy by any stretch of the imagination, but I got the job done. I'd spent enough time watching and helping my mom and dad in the kitchen that

I picked up some things. And those years on my own in California only inspired my creativity.

So, I rolled up my sleeves and got to cooking. While Camp had some standard ingredients at home, I made a couple grocery store runs to supplement.

Not used to cooking with someone else in mind, I planned to make what I enjoyed eating. If Camp liked my food, then fantastic. And if he hated it, that meant there were more leftovers for me.

Late in the afternoon he left the house to run an errand, and I decided to surprise him with dinner. Since I'd spent enough time at the Matheson house growing up, especially around meals, I knew the man ate almost anything. Hopefully, his eating habits hadn't drastically changed in the past eight years.

A half hour after his departure, I got to work pulling out the ingredients. After another thirty minutes of preparation, the dish was ready to go in the oven. I set the timer for an hour. It needed to stay covered for that amount of time and then bake for another twenty minutes uncovered. If my timing worked out as planned, dinner would be on the table by six.

Patting myself on the back for doing something productive, I sat at the kitchen island and spent some time scrolling through social media. I wasn't big on posting about myself, but there were a few friends and influencers I followed. Even when life had been going well for me in California, I barely posted updates. There was no way in hell I'd log on to share the mess I found myself in now.

The people who needed updates heard them directly from me. My circle had always remained small. My parents and Candy received the abbreviated version of my latest drama since I didn't need them worrying about me or changing their plans and rushing back to Dallas to help out. If nothing else, they knew I was safe and sound as Camp's temporary housemate.

What none of them needed to know was how fucking difficult it was holding my feelings in check for the man. Realizing I wasn't the girl anymore who easily gave him shit came as a shock. What made me even more surprised was just how much Camp matured.

He'd always been a hard and diligent worker, in and out of school, but that hadn't stopped the guy from teasing me incessantly. He loved to push my buttons, trying his damnedest to get me to the point where I cussed him out on a weekly basis.

Seemed like both of us had done some growing up since high school. Still, it frustrated the hell outta me for other reasons. The thick layer of annoyance that masked my next-level crush on the man thinned out until there was almost nothing. My walls were crumbling fast, but the abysmal state of my finances kept me from making an impulsive decision. Or else I'd be rushing out of here like my panties were on fire.

The timer went off, pausing my doom scrolling for the moment. I uncovered the dish and reset my timer for another twenty minutes. My mouth watered at the smells filling the space. Distracting myself, I cleaned the dishes and wiped down the counter where I'd done the food preparations. When my timer sounded again, I pulled the sizzling casserole dish out and set it on the stovetop.

My fingers acted on their own, unlocking my phone and sending Camp a message.

> Hey.

> Hey you.

> Are you coming home soon?

> Yeah. Is something wrong? Need anything?

> Nope. Just you.

A series of dots appeared then disappeared, and I wanted to erase my last message.

"What the hell are you doing, Zinn?" I placed the offending device screen-down on the counter and ignored the next few messages coming through. God only knew how he interpreted my last text. I wrung my hands together and considered the best way to play it off when he got back.

Best-case scenario was for Camp to gloss over the whole damn thing like he hadn't just received the most out-of-pocket response from me. Worst-case, he'd come home all cocky with an arsenal of jokes and teasing at the ready.

Fuck, my heart couldn't take it. I was about ready to tuck tail and hide in my room for the rest of the night but decided not to go down like that.

My stomach growled right then, chiding me for even thinking about missing out on the meal I prepared. So, I pulled up my big-girl panties, took down two plates, and grabbed silverware.

On one of my grocery runs, I picked up a bottle of wine and opened it now, hoping the drink would settle my frazzled nerves. *Spoiler alert, it didn't.* But I managed to take a couple of sips before the sound of the door unlocking and opening reached my ears.

I swung around just in time to see Camp's tall and broad form stride over the threshold. We were mid-way through autumn, and, in some ways, summer still lingered in the air with warm weather. Still, Camp wore a thin flannel shirt with the sleeves rolled up to his elbows. His shirt flaps were open, revealing the light blue shirt he had on underneath.

I covered up my blatant appraisal by taking another sip of wine. I had yet to come to grips with how sexy I found him or how he made my body tingle when I least expected it. I didn't need these thoughts taking up space rent-free in my head. *No ma'am!* I had better things to do with my time.

"What smells so good?" The front door was shut, and he strode halfway across the space before I could blink.

Dammit, I shouldn't find his stealthy approach the least bit appealing but alas, there was no hope for me.

This impossible crush was alive and well and dead set on making me sweat my edges out.

"I made dinner." *Duh!*

"Is this the surprise you mentioned?" When the hell had my imagination gotten the best of me? Hearing his tone dip low and sexy had me feeling all kinds of things. My breath caught in my throat, all I could do was nod in response. "What do we have here, Zinn?" With my back to the counter, he stood mere inches away, gazing down at me with a patient look on his stupidly handsome face.

"Uh, nothing special," I stuttered. Mentally chastising myself for acting like some hussy, I figured out how to string another sentence together. "It's Baked Chicken with Peppered Bacon & Wild Rice."

My mind played tricks on me. I swore Camp got closer somehow without moving. A warm puff of air caressed the side of my face as he leaned down and uttered in my ear, "It smells delicious, Zinn. I can't wait to have a taste." *He's not flirting. I repeat. He. Is. Not. Flirting.* I let those words repeat in my head over and over as he straightened. His gaze held mine for a minute before he opened his mouth again. "I'll go wash my hands and be right back."

I am straight-up losing it. When the hell did manners and proper hygiene become so hot that my panties got a little wet? Fanning myself with a dish towel, I watched Camp's tall frame as he disappeared down the hall and into his bedroom. Needing something to distract myself from thoughts of following him and offering myself for dessert, I turned around and spooned a generous helping of the fragrant rice dish on my plate.

It wasn't long before Camp returned to the kitchen, his flannel shirt long gone. His slight tan and muscled arms on full display in a sleeveless shirt. Food forgotten, I watched him rub his hands together while licking his lips in anticipation. Now, more than anything, I wished I were bold enough to offer myself up as the main course.

I shook the thought away the second it popped into my head. Or tried to.

Stop daydreaming! He's your best friend's twin brother and has only ever treated you well because of her, more or less tolerating your behind. Nothing like the cold, hard truth to snuff out my one-sided desire.

Common sense restored, I filled the silence. "Help yourself. I also opened a bottle of wine, if you're interested."

"Oh, I'm most definitely interested." Our gazes clashed, but I glanced away first for self-preservation purposes. It wouldn't do me any good to misinterpret each sentence to come outta his mouth. *Everything is not meant to be sexual innuendo, Zinn! Nor an indecent proposal.*

With my plate and wine glass in hand, I hightailed it over to the dining room table and sat down. I quickly took another sip of wine to calm my nerves without a second thought to my almost empty stomach. Camp was one step ahead of me, though. He entered the room with a plate full of food in one hand and an empty glass along with the bottle of wine in the other. I wasn't sure if I wanted to thank him or cuss him out for enabling my inner lush.

Trying my best to ignore the somersaults happening in my tummy, I scooped food onto my fork and finally got a taste of my hard-earned work.

"Mm." Surprised at how good it turned out this time, I shoveled more into my mouth, uncaring how greedy I looked.

"This is amazing, Zinn."

"It really is."

He chuckled at my immediate reply. Being on the receiving end of compliments felt like some kind of chore, so ever since I was little, I liked to spice them up and always had a flippant response at the ready. People either found it funny or thought I was conceited.

"Are you excited to start your new job?" Camp changed the subject, and I couldn't have been happier.

"Yeah, I've never liked being idle."

"Oh, I remember." The amused tone of his voice had me narrowing my eyes at him. About to ask what he meant by that, my question got cut off when he tacked on a follow-up.

"This another library job then?"

"It is..." Luckily, I'd found a thirty-hour a week position at a community college library. Some days I'd have opening hours and others I would be responsible for closing. I was excited to get back in the swing of things since I loved the atmosphere of libraries, but sometimes it felt like I missed out somehow.

"Have you ever thought about applying to Library School and becoming a Librarian?"

My fork fell, clanking against the half-empty plate.

My eyebrows lifted in shock, and I gazed at the man like I was seeing him for the first time in my life. "The average person doesn't know about Library School, how come you do?"

Camp shrugged his shoulders. "Why are you so surprised that I know things?"

"I don't know. Most people just assume that everyone who works in a library is a librarian. Not many people realize that a master's degree is required."

"Guess I'm an exception then. Now, stop evading my question. Have you considered it?"

"I have..." Something always held me back in the past few years, though. Maybe now was the perfect time to really think over my options and plan for the future.

Picking up my fork, I pushed the remaining food around the plate as my mind wandered. Camp remained silent across from me, but I could feel his eyes on me every once and a while. *What does he see when he looks at me?* I wondered.

My life felt like such an epic mess right now, it wasn't even funny. But Camp came through for me at my worst hour, offering a place to stay. No questions asked. No ulterior motive that I could see. Hell, the man hadn't even asked me to pay rent.

My bad luck turned in the blink of an eye, so why not dream big for once in my life?

"Thanks, Camp." His chestnut brown gaze landed on me. "For what?"

"For everything. For answering my call out of the blue. For helping me when you didn't have to. For letting me move into your home and invade your space. I could go on."

"Zinn, I don't need you to thank me. We've known each other for a long time. I wasn't gonna leave you stranded. Plus, if Candy and my parents found out I didn't help you, they would kill me and hide the body. You're family." His deep, intense stare seared me as he said the last part. "Seriously, though, I would do anything for you, Zinnia."

I gasped, my heart galloping.

"Camp..."

His chair scraped against the accent rug underneath the table as he suddenly stood up. He topped off our glasses before lifting his empty plate. "I'm getting seconds. Do you need anything from the kitchen?"

"I'll take a little more, thanks." Passing my plate, I watched as he spun around and damn near scurried away like something *or someone* followed hot on his heels.

"What's gotten into him?" I wondered out loud. Shaking my head, my thoughts returned to Camp's earlier questions. There were a few things to think about. For the first time in forever, it seemed as though I had the time and space to do so. And it was thanks to Camp. Even though he didn't want it, I would make sure he knew how much his support was appreciated every chance I got.

Chapter Six

My first week at the new job ended on a good note. The Friday shift was short, ending the workday at one o'clock in the afternoon. I decided to treat myself for a change, stopping at the mall and catching a matinee movie.

Enjoying a small popcorn and fountain drink, I sat back and allowed the mountain of stress to drop from my shoulders. Although moving back to Dallas had been a last-minute decision, I knew that all would be well. I just needed to take it one day at a time, putting one foot in front of the other.

On the drive home, my brain circled back to the question Camp posed about the idea of Library School. Pursuing a master's degree in library science held space in the back of my mind for years now, but something kept me from making decisive moves to apply. With a bit more freedom and flexibility in my work schedule, I could take a leap of faith.

I vowed to not let inconsequential things and self-doubt get in my way. Becoming a professional librarian was an obtainable goal. All I had to do was take a chance and reach for it.

Feeling extra motivated, I unlocked the front door and practically floated into the house. Camp standing in the kitchen caught my eye. *A tall drink of water having a tall drink of water.* I shook the thought from my head and almost made the turn down the hallway to escape my overactive libido.

"Hey. Had a good day at work?"

"I did. I had a half-day schedule, so I hung out at the mall for a bit. How was your day?"

"Not too bad. I just put in an offer for my next flip. Now, I wait to hear back from my realtor."

"That's exciting. Congrats!"

"Thanks." His lips spread into a handsome smile that made my knees weak. I decided to get back to my escape plan, but the next words out of his mouth stopped me in my tracks. "Some people from high school are meeting up tonight. Wanna join me?"

Besides Candy, I hardly stayed in touch with folks from school except the random social media post here and there. It might be nice to get out and see some familiar faces. I couldn't keep hiding out at Camp's place forever. Before leaving California, the plan was to finally get some semblance of a social life. And that reminded me, I needed to follow up on Violet's recommendation and contact the chapter leader here in Dallas for the Plucking Ladies Garden Club. I'd decided to reach out to Jessamine Ruella Roe as soon as possible.

"Sure, why not? What time does it start?"

"Most people try to show up around eight or nine."

My gaze moved over to the microwave, noting it was close to six o'clock, so I had plenty of time to get ready.

"Okay. I'll hang out in my room for a bit and then hop in the shower, if that's alright…"

"Yeah, of course." He nodded. "The bar they chose is across town, so let's plan to leave around eight."

"Sounds good. I'll be ready by then."

"Great. I'll probably fix myself a snack. You want anything, Zinn?"

"Nah, I'm good. I ate at the mall earlier. I might get something at the bar later, though."

"Go rest then."

I jerked my head in agreement and booked it down the hallway to my bedroom.

Things were finally looking up. The last of my stuff arrived with little fanfare. There was a roof over my head, and a place I felt safe in. The first week of my new job had gone well.

For a while there, it felt like I'd bitten off more than I could chew. Moving back to Dallas had not gone at all like my plans, but I rallied. Now, life was moving in a positive direction. Hopeful, I decided to grab any moment of happiness and peace offered to me. And recently, Camp remained at the front of my mind when it came to feeling safe and secure. My crush had grown wings and taken flight.

In these past few weeks, I've seen the type of man Camp had become, and I was impressed as hell. Not completely surprised, though. He and Candy were blessed with amazing role models for parents. Although my own parents also raised me right, that didn't stop the fear and doubt from creeping in and taking up real estate.

I had a good head on my shoulders, but sometimes I couldn't escape those moments where it felt like I was drowning in a sea of mediocrity.

Before I knew it, the alarm I'd set to keep me honest chimed at a quarter past seven. It was time to hop in the shower and see some old friends.

Twenty minutes later, I stood in front of my bedroom closet. Fresh, clean, and properly moisturized, I considered my options for a low-key night out. Since the last thing I had any business doing was stunting, I chose a cute, denim shirtdress that hit right above my knees. I paired the outfit with dark-brown, lace-up booties. Bookish stud earrings and my favorite amethyst bracelet completed the look.

Looking good, feeling good. A tiny smile graced my lips as I considered my reflection in the mirror. Before leaving the bedroom, I applied Vaseline and added a dollop of shiny lip gloss on top, tossing the small tubes into the clutch that held the few items I wanted to carry with me.

At eight on the dot, I strutted out of the bedroom, the heels adding extra sway to my hips.

Camp waited for me almost in the exact spot I'd left him earlier. I drank in the sight of him. He also showered and put some effort into his choice of clothing for tonight. Even from behind, he looked amazing in a pair of jeans and a long-sleeve shirt. A light dusting of hair showed on his forearms since he had the sleeves rolled up.

Letting another quiet moment pass, I closed my eyes and took a calming breath before exhaling. "I'm ready," I finally said, alerting him to my presence.

Camp slowly turned to face me, and my body tightened. Almost strangling the clutch in my hand, I focused on unclenching and tried my damnedest to relax.

"You look great, Zinn."

"Thanks. You don't look too bad yourself."

"Aw shucks, darlin'. Ya gonna make a man blush with a compliment like that," he teased, thickening his drawl so much that I wanted to dive in and get lost in his voice.

I chuckled to cover up the thirsty thoughts in my head.

"You play too much, Camp." I shook my head. "Ready to go or what?"

"Let's roll."

Camp secured the front door while my feet automatically carried me to his truck parked in the driveway. Two beeps came from the imposing vehicle and the locks disengaged. Before I lifted my hand to grab the passenger side handle, Camp was already there opening the door.

I glanced over my shoulder. He was so close that the sandalwood fragrance of his cologne reached my nostrils before I could even smother down the urge to take a good, long sniff. "Thank you." My tone softened, taking on a shy and flirty quality even to my own ears. *Fuck, I hope he doesn't hear it.*

"My pleasure, Zinn."

My gaze followed him as he jogged around the front of his truck until he opened his door and his tall, wide frame slid into the driver's seat.

"It'll take us about thirty minutes to get there, I think."

"Cool." I got comfortable as Camp started the car, his radio already tuned to a soft rock station. We were on the road in no time.

Low-key, I was more than happy for Camp to maneuver through crazy-ass Dallas traffic. I'd forgotten how reckless Texas drivers could be even though I'd grown up here. *And don't get me started on the speed limit.* Most people took those signs as a suggestion and not the rule. So, I sat back and tapped my feet to the music, sometimes singing along under my breath.

"We should go to karaoke." His random proposal sliced through the quiet of the cab.

I chuckled. "What? Where did that idea come from?"

"You have a good voice." He shrugged. "I thought you might find something like that fun."

"Maybe. I've never done it before."

"Well then, we'll have to change that soon."

"Whatever you say, Camp." My cheeks twitched with a smile. Turning my head, I glanced out the window and allowed the butterflies in my stomach to flutter with joy and wild abandon. No more than ten minutes later, Camp turned into a large parking lot and found a spot.

The time for fantasies had ended, so I shut that shit down and focused on what lay ahead. A high school reunion of sorts. At least for me because I hadn't laid eyes on a lot of these people since graduation.

"You ready?"

Not really. "Yup," I responded instead, hoping Camp couldn't see past the innocent lie.

We opened our doors at the same time, and I hopped out. I met him in front of the truck, and he stayed close to my side as we made our way to the bar entrance. *A blessing and a curse.* His proximity eased the jitters inside me while at the same time causing flutters around my heart. It was a bitch of a conundrum, this ever-present duality.

I hadn't figured out what to do about it back in high school, so I'd succumbed to my fate and just said fuck it. As long as I kept these feelings to myself, then there was no harm, no foul.

Too bad life had a funny way of shitting on the best laid plans.

Chapter Seven

The cacophony of loud conversations and the jukebox in the corner synched to the speaker system greeted us upon entering Jesse's Tavern. The establishment was already crowded. It was a popular spot for locals and visitors alike. They had an awesome beer selection, good food options, and enough space to accommodate anyone looking to decompress from the stress of adulting.

"Wanna get a drink first?" I stared down at Zinnia, my arm wrapping around her waist to bring her close to me.

She nodded. "Sounds good. I'm a little hungry too." She patted her stomach, a shy smile playing on her shiny lips as she peered up at me.

Fuck, she was beautiful. *And mine.* There was no chance in hell I'd allow more than a few inches to come between us tonight. Common sense and my plans be damned. A quick scan of the place had my hackles on high alert, the protective side of me locked and loaded. I had already noticed too many lecherous gazes aimed at my girl, and I wanted to pummel every single bastard who dared to look her way. The possessive beast inside me wanted to let every motherfucker in here know that she was ours.

"Let's order and then we can find the group."

We hadn't taken two steps before a hand clamped onto my shoulder. "Yo, Matheson!"

The voice of one of my best friends broke through the din of noise and my one-track mind. Squeezing Zinn's side, I stopped our forward motion and turned around to greet Quentin Cole.

"Your girl let you out of the house this time?"

"Fuck you very much, C. And yeah, she did actually." We chuckled at the ribbing. Forcing myself to drop my hold of Zinnia temporarily, I pulled Quentin into a quick hug, pounding his back.

Quentin's gaze moved to the right of me, and I saw the moment his curiosity and interest landed on my girl. He stepped back and got a full look at her.

"Zinnia Whitfield!" His booming exclamation scraped against my eardrum. If I didn't know he was happily attached to someone, I would've already wrapped my arm around Zinn and pulled her back against my side.

"Hey, Quentin. Good to see you."

"You too. How long's it been? Eight years? How are you?"

I listened to their exchange, watching the play of emotions cross her pretty features. "I guess it's been about that long. I'm good. How've you been?"

"Can't complain. Life is going pretty damn well for me actually."

"Glad to hear that," my girl said, giving my best friend the sweetest and most sincere smile.

Like me, my core group of friends were stand-up guys, so I knew not to worry about Quentin being around Zinnia. He'd never intentionally screw up the life he was building with his fiancée or our friendship. Hell, the man was my go-to electrician whenever the project became too advanced for my skill set. And if I knew one thing about Quentin Cole, he wasn't about to mess with his money either.

"Where's everybody sitting?" Q asked once their catch-up came to a pause.

I gestured over my shoulder toward a back corner where I noticed the growing group.

"We were just about to grab drinks, order food, and head over when you arrived."

"Copy." Q slapped my shoulder on the way past me as he muscled through the crowd.

"Guess he's thirsty," Zinn muttered, not hiding her sarcasm. I chuckled, shaking my head at how his mode switched so easily.

"You could say that." Without second-guessing my actions, I circled fingers around Zinn's wrist before taking her hand once again, swearing I felt her pulse jump. Her small hand fit perfectly in mine. I got us moving again, winding through the throng of bodies and making sure to hold on tightly to my girl. Now that I had her with me, the plan was to never let her go.

We stepped up to the bar right as one of the three bartenders passed a pint toward Q. Using my tall and wide stature for good and evil, I gave Zinn just enough space to wiggle up to the counter in front of me while I glued myself to her back. My gaze fell on one of the laminated menus, so I grabbed it and placed it in front of her.

"Thanks," she whispered, peeking over her shoulder at me. My imagination almost got the best of me. I thought about leaning down and demanding that she show her thanks another way but wrestled down the urge.

Forcing my gaze over to the line of taps behind the bar, I felt the weight of Q's stare on me. I did my best to ignore his nosy ass for a moment before splitting my attention his way.

"What?" I muttered under my breath.

"Oh nothing. I'm just seeing my old friend in a new light, is all." The smug bastard chuckled at my expense. He knew and saw too much. I could wring his neck, but the move would require me to break contact with Zinn. Something well beyond my capabilities at the moment.

As loud conversations buzzed and random bodies closed in around us, a desperate need slammed into me. My skin heated at our contact already, but dammit if it was even remotely enough. Every part of me ached, especially my not-so patient dick.

Unable to deny myself any longer, I bent my head and rested my lips against the shell of her left ear in the guise of making sure she could hear me over the noise. The sweetest gasp left her lips as I felt a shiver zip through her petite frame. Every muscle inside me twitched, wanting to cause the same reaction in her again and again.

My breath coasted over the sensitive bit of flesh before I asked, "What looks good to you, Zinn?"

"Um, yeah. I think I'll get an order of buffalo wings and fries."

"Sounds good. And what do you wanna drink?"

"I'll get a Long Island Iced Tea, please."

I got the attention of one of the bartenders and placed the order, tacking on a few additions of my own. Letting them know we would join our group in the corner when it came time to deliver the food, we each took our drinks. Bodies crowded around us, vying to catch the eye of a bartender, so we turned from the bar counter and made the trip toward our group.

Again, I didn't give Zinnia the time or option to reject my touch as we navigated through the clusters of people standing in our path. Quentin led the way, probably eager to sit down with his beer. I was right there with him.

Finally, our trio arrived at the back corner and sidled up to the group of high school friends. Hopefully, Zinnia recognized some familiar faces and didn't feel disengaged or too far removed. I saw these people at least a few times a year, so a round of greetings for me and Q started as everyone's attention moved to us.

Maddie Thompson coordinated tonight's meetup, and it was her who noticed Zinnia beside me first. "Zinnia!" she exclaimed.

"Hey! It's so good to see y'all." Unable to resist temptation, all of my focus fell on her while her face beamed with the prettiest smile.

The group shuffled around to make room for us. Seeing the perfect spot for two, I guided Zinnia to one end of the booth. Without blinking an eye, I sat right next to her and Quentin took the chair across from us.

Conversations continued around us, Maddie grabbing Zinn's attention and pelting her with endless questions. Most friends from high school knew that she moved out of state for college, but I figured not many had learned of her return now. Except for her family and mine, I doubted that she let the masses know her business like that. Since I've known her, she'd kept things relatively close to her chest. Remembering how she'd turned to me in her moment of crisis sent a lightning bolt to my chest. She needed me, and nothing would've stopped me from being there for her and helping in whatever way I could.

Even now, I wanted to become her rock. Her confidant. Her safe place. The position of best friend had already been claimed by my twin sister, but I had always wished we were closer and nicer to each other in our younger years. And those parts of my dream were slowly becoming reality since her return to Dallas.

Coming to the realization that Zinnia's attention focused elsewhere for the time being, I turned to my best friend for a bit of distraction. And as soon as I caught his knowing stare, I thought about inserting myself into whatever other conversation happened nearby.

His teeth gleamed, his smile was so big. I could tell what the man was thinking before anything came out his mouth. And I gave him every nonverbal warning to keep his trap shut while Zinnia was within earshot.

"Do you know if Hill and Rob are coming tonight?" I asked for something to say. We didn't usually beat around the bush with each other but today had to be some kind of exception. Things were going so well between us that I didn't want even a bit of light teasing to fuck up what we had going on.

"Guess your memory's been squarely on other priorities lately. Hill is on vacation with his boyfriend, and Rob is at a work conference." Q shared the information and then took a drink from his pint.

"Oh, that's right. Must've slipped my mind."

"I bet." Again, a smug look crossed his face, and I almost kicked him under the table.

"Looking for my next project has taken up a lot of my time. Just started the closing period."

"Congrats, C. Think you're gonna need my services with this one?"

"More than likely. I'll let you know as soon as I can."

"Bet."

Quentin was a damned good electrician, having gone to trade school a year after graduation. Like me, he'd worked construction through high school and found his calling with electrical work. When a particular project surpassed my limited wiring abilities, I consulted Quentin and paid him well for the expertise.

Noticing the moment he was fixing to open his mouth to interrogate or tease me again about Zinn, I beat him to the punch. "Is everything good with Jazz?"

His face lit up at the mention of his favorite subject. His pregnant fiancée. "Yeah, man. She called me right before I walked in to remind me to stop by the store to pick up some stuff for her." He chuckled, taking another gulp of his beer.

"So, that's the real reason she let you outta the house."

"Har har har, smart ass."

I raised a brow. "Is it a lie, though?"

Ignoring my question, he shared, "Her cravings are getting hella wild, man!" Q shook his head.

"What is it now?" I loved hearing my best friend's stories, low-key cataloging any and all information for when it became my turn. A quick glance at Zinn told me she was still chatting and enjoying herself. My girl needed to get out more. I'd make sure to give her some subtle nudges after tonight.

"C... She be asking for the weirdest shit now, man." I turned my head and focused on my conversation with Quentin.

Intrigued, I leaned forward. Elbows on the table. Invested.

"Don't leave me in suspense, Q."

"Ice cream and pickles." Quentin visibly shuddered, face contorting with a level of disgust that sent me falling against the backrest of the booth and laughing. Hard.

"Yeah, that's - uh - an interesting combination."

"It's nasty as hell is what it is."

"Maybe you should see if there's pickle-flavored ice cream out there. Two birds and all that."

"Oh hell no!"

I got another good laugh at his expense. "You better suck it up, buttercup. You're the main reason she's in this condition."

"Yeah, I know." A look of pure pride filled his face. And a pang of jealousy smacked me right in the chest. I longed for late-night grocery runs simply to satisfy my girl. Her asking me for anything and everything because she knew I'd travel to the ends of the earth just to make her happy.

I couldn't resist taking another glance at the woman by my side. This time, though, her gaze connected with my greedy one.

"Hey." She leaned toward me with a small smile.

"Hey," I cleared my suddenly dry throat and returned the greeting.

"You think our food is coming out soon?"

"Probably. I can go up and check." Already moving before I finished the sentence, I noticed a harried server heading in our direction. Instead of sitting back down, I walked toward the woman to help.

"This order for Campbell?"

The server listed off our two orders of buffalo wings, fries, and mozzarella sticks which were all placed on the round serving tray.

"Yep, that's for us. Let me lighten your load a bit."

I grabbed two loaded plates from the tray and turned back to the table, my eyes zeroing in on Zinn immediately. Her face lit up as she watched my approach. Realizing the hungry look in her eyes was meant for the food and not me would be enough to give a lesser man a complex. Good thing I already knew I had my work cut out for me when it came to her.

Soon, her ravenous looks would be mine alone. I'd make it my new mission in life.

Once all the food got served and placed on the table in front of us, I let my girl dig in first. She grabbed a plate of the buffalo wings for herself but left the fries and mozzarella sticks between our trio. Knowing he didn't need an invitation, Q plucked a stick from the plate closest to him, and I watched as he shoved the appetizer in his mouth and promptly burned his tongue.

It's what his greedy ass deserves, I thought to myself.

Like Zinn, I started with the buffalo wings and fries while letting the mozzarella sticks cool down a bit. In less than twenty minutes, all four plates were practically licked clean. Zinn wasn't afraid of chowing down even in front of a big group. A trait I didn't realize I'd appreciate about her until now.

Bumping her shoulder, I asked, "Satisfied?"

"Oh, definitely."

"Ready for another drink?"

"Yeah, one more is fine. Otherwise you might have to carry me outta here."

"I wouldn't mind," I whispered next to her ear, giving her a wink after slightly leaning away. The dim lighting in the bar and Zinn's dark complexion couldn't hide her blush. *Hell yeah! That's what I like to see.* With that, I stood up to return to the bar. Quentin followed, giving the excuse of also needing a refill, but I could see right through his bullshit.

"You got it bad, C." A hand clamped around my left shoulder as we weaved our way through the crowd. It seemed like twice as many people were there after barely an hour had passed since our arrival.

"I'm well aware. And your point is?" Right as we came up, a glorious spot opened up at the bar top.

"Okay, I see how it is, bro. Does this mean you're finally taking your shot with her?"

I nodded and then followed up with, "I am."

"Well, it's about damned time." Quentin delivered another two slaps to my back. His way of showing his support, I guessed.

Neither of us got to say anything more since a bartender noticed us and hustled right over. I ordered drinks for me and Zinn while Quentin asked for a second beer. We paid and settled our tabs. Hands full, I turned away from the bar and immediately felt a nudge. Quentin waved his ringing phone in my face and gestured toward the entrance. Giving him a nod, I returned my sights to the corner where our group of friends chatted away. Less than ten minutes had passed, but I was eager to lay eyes on my girl again.

Quentin's observation was spot on, although his words didn't truly capture the urgency pumping through my bloodstream.

Yeah, I had it bad. These feelings had grown exponentially since high school, even in her absence.

And the tethers of my control were disintegrating at an alarming rate with our extended contact. It couldn't be helped. My plan to continue at a slow and steady pace was about to go up in smoke, and there wasn't a damned thing I could do to stop it.

Aw well. As long as I get my girl...

A shit-eating grin stretched my face until I got closer to the table. And then my blood boiled as my vision went hazy with rage.

Someone wanted to die tonight. *Scratch that. This bastard is already dead,* the beast inside me growled with a resolute promise.

No one messed with my Zinn and got away with it.

Chapter Eight

My skin flushed with heat as the ground shifted under my feet. I touched my cheeks and immediately felt their warmth. His response and that wink about did me in. Cartoon hearts in my eyes, I followed his retreating back until both him and Quentin got swallowed up by the loitering crowd of drinkers.

A few minutes of peace were beyond my reach, though. The moment they were out of sight it felt like I could breathe normally again, but that relief was short-lived, however. Because Alec Dickerson decided it was the perfect time to slink over and steal the seat next to me. Camp's seat. I cringed, skin cooling with his unwanted attention. Something about Alec always rubbed me the wrong way. Not much had changed since high school either. Hell if it didn't get worse somehow, since the guy seemed like more of a douche canoe than before.

Once the food arrived, my hunger took over and I dug into the late meal with gusto. I'd listened to the conversations around with half an ear and could only vaguely recall when Alec joined the group.

"It's a nice surprise to see you here, Zinnia." My skin crawled at the way he added emphasis to my name.

"Oh, why's that?"

"I hadn't heard you were back in town."

Why would you? I thought to myself. "Moved back recently," I shared, keeping my responses brief and tone curt hardly seemed to discourage him, though.

"Guess you just weren't cut out for California, huh?"

What the actual fuck? I gave him some stink-eye as he aimed a fake, smarmy smile in my direction.

I could, in fact, believe how much of a prick he was being to me right then, so I didn't see the point in cussing his pretentious, rude ass out like I wanted.

"If that's what you want to tell yourself." I was beyond proud of myself for going away to school, earning my degree, and working at a university for a few years. This prick wasn't capable of diminishing my experiences or my truth.

"Don't be like that, Zinnia." He scooted closer, boxing me in. When I felt a soft tap on my left shoulder, I turned to Maddie and saw the question and concern in her eyes. *You okay?* she mouthed. I nodded and shifted my body towards her and the rest of the group, hoping that Alec would take the hint.

Spoiler alert, he didn't.

"So, are you seeing anyone right now, Zinnia?"

Something was definitely wrong with this guy. A little unhinged, maybe. His close proximity made me wish I was somewhere else. Anywhere else. I should've followed Camp to the bar. Hindsight was twenty-twenty.

But luck appeared to be on my side. One thought of Camp summoned the man, bringing him back into my line of sight. And the way the crowd parted as he barreled toward our group was a sexy image to behold. It also felt like some shit was about to go down. This wouldn't end well especially if Alec continued to act like an ass. Because, for as long as I'd known him, Camp has had a protective streak a mile and a half long. And it had always extended to me due to my best friend status with his twin sister. Sometimes I felt lucky and grateful to be included and other times not so much. Right now, I wasn't sure what to feel, except for trepidation and need. A fire blazed in those chestnut-colored eyes. I followed his approach much like a spooked deer. I sat there frozen, unable to break outta these sudden feelings that had me in a chokehold.

We'd known each other for more than a decade, my crush persisting almost that entire time. And nowhere in my bank of memories did I recall a more severe look from him. His nostrils flared. Tracing his handsome facial features, my gaze zoomed in on the noticeable tick in his jaw. If this were a cartoon, steam would be coming outta his ears right about now.

Camp stopped behind the chair Quentin claimed earlier, his eyes narrowed at the guy currently in his spot. My back straightened at the not-so subtle disturbance in the air. At the wave of hostility wafting off of him. Camp was pissed. And coming to that conclusion required nothing more than a quick glance in his direction. But Alec wasn't the brightest bulb; I remembered as much from high school.

He stood there wordlessly for the longest minute. As if he'd put every bit of energy into placing our drinks on the table in a calm manner. Any civility fled after that, though.

His gaze didn't stray from my unwelcomed seatmate. Another peek at Alec let me know that he was worse than a prick. He was an idiot itching for a fight, going by the dickish smirk riding his thin lips. And Camp would gladly oblige him.

"You're in my seat." The statement was more growl than anything. My forearms had goosebumps while I squeezed my thighs together. Two completely different bodily reactions to this new and foreboding version of my best friend's brother rushed me in that moment.

"Now Campbell, don't you think you've monopolized enough of Zinnia's time tonight? It's my turn to catch up with her."

His turn? "I'm not some kinda toy here for your enjoyment, Alec." I wanted to throat-punch this asshole. With the fierce look in Camp's eyes, he might just do it for me. But I couldn't let that happen, right?

I refused to allow the first night we hung out together with old friends end in assault. Although Alec needed to learn his lesson by getting his ass beat, I didn't want Camp getting in trouble.

"What the hell did you just say, asshole?"

"You heard me." Alec turned to me and asked, "Are you seeing anyone right now, Zinnia?" *As if I'd give him the time of day after all of this nonsense.*

Before I fixed my mouth to reject him with every breath in my lungs, Camp moved in a flash and yanked Alec up by his collar. My body responded on autopilot, heart thundering as too many images flashed in my mind. Every thought was on Camp and what would happen if he threw the first punch.

"You can hardly blame me for asking, Campbell. I mean I just want to try her out once since I've never had a black girl before." His abhorrent statement brushed across my skin like a burst of frigid air and then it was gone. Alec, the asshole, mattered very little to me so his comments were insignificant at the end of the day, but Campbell was another matter altogether. I worried about him and this temper I was coming to find out was somewhat volatile. The muscles in his forearm strained as the fist tightened around Alec's collar. He pulled the stupid bastard, yanking him closer until their faces were only centimeters apart. I held my breath waiting for something. Disaster to strike. Camp to come to his senses and realize Alec's dumbass wasn't worth an arrest record.

"You'll never fucking touch her."

But holding my breath and my tongue wasn't gonna do a damned thing if fists started flying.

"Camp. Camp!" I tried to grab his laser-focused attention. When I shouted his name a second time, the chestnut gaze I adored turned to me and sent my heart galloping as my core gushed.

With the ferocious look in his eyes, I knew he wasn't going to let this go easily, but I still had to try. Something. Anything to defuse the situation.

"He's not worth this, Camp. Will you let him go and then we can just leave?" I'd rather us end the night early than see this situation play out. My focus stayed on Camp, but I wondered why no one from our group moved to de-escalate things. Dammit, I wanted to leap over the table and knock some sense into him. And then maybe climb him like a tree afterwards.

Now is not the time for these freaky thoughts of yours, my inner voice reminded me. Shaking my head, I made another attempt at ending the intense situation.

"I'm ready to go home, Camp. Let's go, okay?"

"Yeah, Camp. How about you listen to your bitch and call it a night, huh?"

My hand moved as if it had its own brain. I clutched Camp's wrist, hoping to break through the rage I sensed coming to a head. Alec had a death wish. There was no other reason for him to spew the vitriol he did. But that was the least of my worries.

Alec goaded him on purpose and for reasons unknown. And there wasn't much I could do to stop Camp from pummeling his face in from my current spot. Boxed in and helpless, I ran out of ideas.

I saw the exact moment Camp decided to shut him up for good, and my stomach lurched. Any words spoken by me seemed to add fuel to the raging blaze, so I kept my mouth shut. But watching as Camp twisted his body and lifted his other fist sent fear piercing through my chest.

My body parts moved on their own. First, the hand holding onto his wrist clamped down harder, hoping to ground him somehow. My feet lifted as if I was getting ready to jump over the table and insert myself between these two men.

What the actual fuck, Zinn? I stopped myself, too many thoughts and scenarios running through my head in that split second. I'd already tried to de-escalate the situation to no avail. And there was no way putting my ass in between two grown men itching to fight would end well. So, I forced myself to release the useless hold on Camp and let go. This battle was all about their manly egos and less about me.

Still, I couldn't stop watching in horror as Camp's other fist came close to connecting with Alec's stupid face.

In the nick of time, Quentin broke through the crowd, clocked the explosive situation, and rushed over.

"Woah, woah, what the hell is going on with y'all?" Instead of grabbing Camp from behind, he got in the middle, pushing them apart. I breathed a little easier with Quentin back. I didn't want to think about what was fixing to happen if he returned even a few seconds later.

"Get your friend on a fucking leash, Q, because he's lost his damned mind."

"If you don't shut your mouth, asshole, I'll do it for you."

"Eh, calm the fuck down, the both of you." Quentin's focus whipped back and forth, trying to figure out what the hell happened in his absence.

"Alec, you need to go back to wherever the hell you came from and quit crowding Zinnia."

The pompous ass tried to fix his mouth to refuse the smart advice given the volatile situation.

"That wasn't a fucking suggestion, Alec. Best believe C would be handing you your ass right now if I wasn't here. Just be lucky I came back to the table when I did."

"Fuck you. Whatever."

Spitting out his last retort, Alec shuffled away from their side of the table, pushed past Quentin, and knocked against Camp's shoulder. Thankfully, Quentin still had a grip on Camp's arm or else he might've finished where they left off.

Now that I finally could escape, I rushed out of my spot. Quentin made room for me to walk right up to Camp.

Trapped in a feedback loop of fear and worry and anger, the only words I could find to say were, "I wanna go home."

It took a few moments for my statement to break through Camp's heavy cloud of rage. At this point, I wasn't sure if any of that was about me. And right then I could care less. I was done. With male ego. With high school nonsense. Done with bullies and Alec's stupid ass. And I was also done with Camp and his unexpected violent temper.

Lies, girl. You know you found that shit hot as all hell just now. I ignored the know-it-all voice in my head telling every single one of my secrets. An altercation was not the way I figured our night would end, and I still wrapped my head around Camp's actions.

Muscles in his jaw ticked once...twice before he licked his lips and opened his mouth. "Okay, we can go."

Leaving the drinks and barely waving goodbye to the few remaining people in our party, the three of us made our way to the exit. Once we got outside, I breathed in the cool, night air, hoping that everything else cooled down as well.

Since I led the departure, it took a glance over my shoulder to see that Quentin stayed close behind me while Camp trailed in the rear. He reminded me of a raging bull who didn't get its way. Didn't knock out the ballsy rider who dared to get on his back for eight seconds of glory.

Well, it served him right. Nobody told him to go toe to toe with Alec and hulk out, acting like some caveman. No matter how my core gushed with the sexy-ass display, the whole thing had been unnecessary.

I reached for the handle of the passenger-side door, but Quentin stopped the move by sliding in front of me and leaning on the door in question.

"I'm not in the mood."

"Copy that. But hear me out for a second." Since Camp parked the truck under a lamp post I could see Quentin's eyes clearly. I decided to hear what he had to say.

"I'm listening."

"Don't be too angry at C, okay? He would go to war for you any day. No matter the reason. Keep that in mind."

He stared at me for several seconds longer, figuring his statements really hit home. Meanwhile my mind raced. Quentin turned and jerked the door open for me. I climbed in and uttered my thanks as an afterthought.

The silence of the cab descended over me while Camp and Quentin had one last exchange outside.

I couldn't hear a word of their conversation and wasn't sure if it mattered if I did. My mind whirred with too many thoughts of my own. Quentin's confusing statement took up most of the space.

He would go to war for you any day.

A minute later, his door opened. Camp got in the driver's seat, cranked the ignition, and reversed out of the parking spot. All without saying a peep.

Without realizing it, my worry and confusion quickly twisted into anger and disappointment. The continued silence in the truck only fed these feelings. And by the time he rolled into his driveway, I was a powder keg ready to blow.

I'd forever be grateful for Camp taking me in like he did. Although I've had a crush on the guy for over a decade, I refused to excuse tonight's behavior. I had to know what the hell happened. And I wouldn't stop until he gave me an answer that made sense.

Because right now nothing did.

Chapter Nine

Like an unspoken rule, the two of us stayed on our best behavior over the last few weeks. We'd shared space like it was the most natural thing for us to do. The toxic and annoying habit of seeing which buttons to push and how far we could get under each other's skin was child's play, and we were no longer children.

My feelings for Zinnia had grown in her absence, but dammit if they hadn't multiplied exponentially having her in such close proximity. I couldn't keep my eyes off of her or my possessiveness in check. All of it was a fucking lost cause, and nothing proved it more than my outburst at the bar.

As the crowd parted and my gaze landed on Zinnia and the bastard daring to sit next to her, my vision blurred. In the heat of the moment, it all got blown straight to hell. Any control I had left. My temper. My common sense. My need to protect and claim my girl reigned supreme. And there was nothing anybody could say to break me from the spell I was under.

My veins still pulsed, blood boiling at the memory of Alec's digs. His obnoxious insinuations. The overt and wildly inappropriate passes he'd flung in Zinnia's direction. Then, he had the balls to sling racist bullshit on top of everything else. At my Zinn. *Mine,* the feral voice inside my head growled with urgency.

Even now, nothing and no one could tell me any differently about how things went down. *I'm just pissed I didn't get to punch the bastard in his filthy mouth.*

Wordlessly, Zinnia jumped out of my truck and marched toward the front door. I watched her unlock it and walk over the threshold before making one move to follow her. Something inside me still crawled its way outward, itching to fight or fuck. And neither of those options seemed likely at this point.

Expecting a deafening silence to greet me, I trudged into my home and secured the door behind me. Turning around, I stopped cold at the vision of Zinnia in the center of the room. She stood there with her arms crossed. Her beautiful and expressive face filled with too many emotions to pinpoint at once.

No matter how much I wanted to stand there and take in every single thing about her, I couldn't. Not right now. Not with the way rage still held me in its clutches. I refused to take these negative feelings out on her.

"What the hell was that, Camp?" But it appeared that Zinnia didn't feel the same way as me.

"Leave it be, Zinn. Please," I forced the plea out through gritted teeth. After thirty minutes of silence on the ride home, my voice sounded low and scratchy. But I had to say something. A last-ditch effort to not fuck this situation up any more than I already had.

"Why did you let him get to you?" Staring into Zinnia's pretty brown eyes, I knew deep down that she wouldn't drop it. She didn't share the same concerns, not wanting to rock the boat we were on. Especially now when everything felt so fucking precarious.

"What? You expect me to sit back and let him disrespect you like that? No fucking chance."

"Camp, he's been an asshole since birth. You should've ignored him. Like I was doing."

"He wasn't getting away with the shit he said to you. I won't apologize for my actions. I only wish I got to knock him on his ass."

"And what was that supposed to solve, huh?"

"Zinn, I don't want to fight with you."

"Oh, so now you don't wanna fight. Could've fooled me. So, what, that was all just some dick measuring contest then? You had to show how much of a man you are protecting the damsel in distress."

"Zinn," I warned. Too bad my girl was on a fucking roll at the moment.

"Well, I can pick a fight too." She closed the distance between us and pushed at my shoulder.

"Don't."

"Don't what, huh? Put hands on you. You had no problem doing it earlier. What's the difference now?'

"I was protecting you, dammit!" I grumbled, making every effort to keep my voice down and not feed into the fire I witnessed in her eyes.

The past three weeks had been blissful torture. *Look but don't touch* was the ever-present adage at the forefront of my mind, day in and day out. I had my dream girl within reach. Moved into my house, for chrissakes. But I couldn't rush. Dared not accelerate my plans or chuck them out the window altogether. Yet, this argument would have all my good intentions go up in a blaze of glory.

"I'm not your sister, Campbell. I don't want or need your protection all the damn time."

Well, screw waiting, I told myself. If this was how it was meant to go down, then who was I to get in the way?

I'm not your sister, Campbell. The statement echoed in my ears, the only thing circling around in my head.

My feet started on their own. Before I knew it, Zinnia and I were moving as one unit. Her words were a catalyst. Maybe she meant them as a punch in the gut, but I only saw them as a reminder. The truest statement ever spoken in the heat of the moment. "You think I don't know that," I said. There was no point holding it in any longer. "I know damn well who you are and what you mean to me." *What you've always meant to me.*

Those pretty eyes widened at my guttural tone. "Camp..." She stuttered over my name while stumbling backwards. The cat was out of the bag now. I wouldn't stop my approach the same way I couldn't stop the confession from spilling out. This moment was inevitable. Unavoidable.

"You have no idea, do you?" A look of confusion crossed her face, and I knew. She had no fucking clue what can of worms her prodding opened.

Before her back hit the edge of the island, I wrapped an arm around her waist and took the brunt of the impact. Despite how adamant she was about not needing my protection, it was ingrained in me.

"Protecting you has fuck-all to do with treating you like my sister or her best friend."

A hitched breath forced my gaze down to her mouth. A mouth I dreamed about claiming in every way for over a decade. Since resistance was no longer part of my vocabulary, I raised my right hand and traced her lips with the pad of my thumb. "You have the most tempting mouth, Zinn." Especially when she gave me shit.

This close, she couldn't hide anything from me. I saw it all. Her face was an open book that I refused to put down. I wanted to discover and reveal each one of her secrets tucked within the pages until I knew everything about her. And she learned everything about me. I wanted our stories to blend into an epic tale of love and friendship. Passion and possession.

As if she could read my mind, her lips parted in shock. I crowded closer, unable to resist my feelings for one more second. "You can't be–"

Caging her in, I bent my arms and leaned down to hold her gaze. "Can't what?"

"You can't be serious. You don't like me that way."

"The hell I don't," I immediately cut in. "I would've claimed you back in high school if I didn't know you'd roast my ass."

Zinn's gaze held mine, searching for something that stared her right in the face even though she made every attempt not to believe it.

"Camp, stop teasing me already."

"What makes you think anything I've said tonight is a tease, huh?" She shook her head in denial. My Zinn was stubborn. "Stop fighting me for once." I had a mind to grab her shoulders and shake some sense into her. "Let me show you how serious I am." *That nothing about this moment is a joke.*

"H-how?" She tripped over the question, the tremor in her voice giving her away. I made her nervous. My body hummed with energy. Excitement. A heavy need that drove me forward and closer to the ultimate prize.

Zinn and I being the end goal.

"Can I?"

Her tongue peeked out and then she nibbled on her bottom lip before straightening her back as much as our positions allowed. A smile teased my own lips as I watched her fidget, noticing the exact moment she tried to erect her protective walls against me. *Well fuck that,* I thought to myself. Because I intended to make it impossible for her to hide from me, literally and figuratively.

Giving her full access to me and mine had always been part of the plan, only now the timeline got pushed up even more. But that couldn't be helped.

"What?!" She arched a dark eyebrow, challenging me with the simple expression. Her sassy attitude knew no bounds, and I loved seeing her direct it at me now. I missed when her fiery personality came to the surface ready to singe me from the inside out. Without a worry or care. Loved when she was no-nonsense and spoke her mind. There was nothing like it, actually.

And it was one of the reasons I fell in love with her the way I did. Craved her with every ounce of my being. With every breath in my lungs. The years and distance only worked to grow these feelings. This passion that was overfilled and damn near about to erupt. Each version of our dynamic appealed to me. Hell, she did it with little to no effort. The soft, sweet, and more mature version of this girl had my protective instincts on high alert. But the spicier tone of hers always got my engine revved up in a way that no other woman managed to do. Discovering new sides to Zinn and the woman she's become would forever be my favorite pursuit. And as long as I finally got to call her mine, I'd be a happy and lucky man.

My ravenous gaze dipped down to her lips before responding to her question. "Kiss you."

"Huh?" Big, brown eyes blinked at me in confusion.

"You heard me," I said, brushing our fronts together. The sound of my pulse thundered in my ears. Even still, I heard Zinn's hitched breath. Felt the way her body shuddered. I crowded in again, stepping into her bubble without a second thought.

"I've wanted to know how you taste for ten years." There was nowhere for her to go. I'd boxed her in. It didn't escape my notice that she wasn't attempting to break away either. She was sucked into this magnetic orbit just as much as me. Just the two of us.

"Camp, I–"

"Say yes," I urged her. "Don't overthink and don't refuse me, Zinn."

Several expressions crossed her face in the span of seconds. I watched and waited as she held a full conversation in her head. It was way past time she came to know my feelings and intentions when it came to her. No more playing the long game. I wanted her. Right here. Right now.

She only had to make the leap and come over to my way of thinking. Because I knew, without a shadow of a doubt, that we were meant for each other. These last few weeks of sharing my home with her cinched it. And there was no going back to the old days when I only held the role of her best friend's brother. It wasn't enough anymore. Hadn't been for a long time now.

Zinn tipped her head back. Her eyes were like windows to her soul, and I had a full and unobstructed view. With every bit of her attention on me, my dick twitched in my boxer briefs. My body felt like a live wire this close to her.

"Do it already." As if she floundered in disbelief at the current sequence of events, her directive dared me to claim her lips the way I so desperately wanted. Only actions would drive the point home for her. Because she still held doubt. It was right there in the dark pools of her brown eyes. She'd pushed against the truth of my words like this was one of the childish games we used to play with each other. Seeing how far we got under each other's skin.

But this wasn't a game for me. And something told me it wasn't one for her either, but she couldn't quite move past our old behaviors.

I leaned forward until our faces were centimeters apart. Close enough to share her breaths. "You said it yourself, Zinn. Just so we're clear. This won't end after one taste. I've waited too long."

Her full lips parted. Was it to curse me or issue another challenge? I wouldn't wait to find out. This time I fulfilled my promise. To her. And to myself. Sealed it with a kiss that did nothing less than rock the ground underneath my feet.

Just like I told her seconds ago. There was no going back after this. She tasted sweeter than ambrosia and the ravenous beast inside had the worst sweet tooth imaginable. She made me a glutton. And when she opened more for me, flicking her tongue against my lips, I knew I wouldn't rest until she screamed my name.

Game on.

Chapter Ten

Punch-drunk. It felt like I'd been submerged in a deep pool of lust and need, inundated with long-held emotions that got new life breathed into them.

An unexpected confirmation that he shared the same feelings as me. He was dangerous to my equilibrium. Always had been. *Always will be.*

Camp claimed my mouth as wholeheartedly as he claimed my heart. His lips drank from mine as if I was his first sip of water after a tough workout. Our bodies were close. So close I refused to imagine going back to a time when he wouldn't hold me like this.

My heart thundered as my core quivered. Even though I tried to fight this earlier, assuming he took one joke a little too far, I'd dreamt of this moment too many times.

The air in the room was thick with tension. Desire. Our focus wrapped in each other to the point that everything else slipped away.

Since this was probably just a case of misplaced energy, I wanted to take as much as he did. Fight or fuck mode. Now that he opened the floodgates, every part of me got on the same page. I'd rather let our bodies do the talking than our mouths. God knew we'd done enough verbal sparring in our youth.

My tongue also wanted in on the action, craving a deeper taste of the man who loved to burrow under my skin. Even after so many years, he lived rent-free in my head. I flicked it against his lips and felt a rumbling sound from Camp. His large hands slid down my back and cupped the cheeks of my ass through my shirtdress. When he squeezed me there, my lips parted in a gasp, and he took the opportunity to dive in more. He plundered my mouth like it belonged to him. Like he was hell-bent on memorizing the taste and feel of me in every corner and crevice.

I moaned at the thought, needing to get closer. My limbs moved on their own, desperate to cling to this man like some spider-monkey. Climbing him like a tree came to mind, so I hitched a leg up with every intention of doing just that. Camp was one step ahead of me, though.

Without missing a beat or putting distance between us, he used his hold on my ass to hoist me up and onto the island counter. My heart skipped the moment he lifted me as if I weighed nothing, which was far from the truth. But Camp was strong enough to do whatever he put his mind to.

My legs wrapped around his waist, desperate to feel him. I was burning up, and he needed to ease the blaze he'd caused inside me. Instead, he nibbled on my bottom lip before pulling out of the kiss.

"You believe me now, baby?"

"Huh?" My brain tried to play catch-up as his question floated between us. His eyes were dark pools that I low-key wanted to drown in. Our heavy breaths mixed and mingled together while his big body still loomed over me.

A knowing, crooked grin spread on his bruised lips and my pussy pulsed at the sight. One charming smirk shouldn't do me in. Or have me ready and willing to spread my thighs for him, but it did. There was no denying how he made me feel. Not anymore.

"If you want me so bad then why did you stop?" I sassed.

Gripping my outer thighs and forcing them open, he stepped between the space he created. My breath stuttered at the boldness. The rizz wafted off him like a thick cloud of smoke.

I'd always thought Camp treated me with a bit of indifference due to my close friendship with his sister. He'd tolerated my presence with quips and butting heads on a weekly, if not daily, basis. How could I have known he harbored similar feelings?

"Is my girl greedy for me?" He growled in this deep, sexy whisper that had me gushing. His lower half brushed against me, and the imprint of his hard-on was evident even through our clothes. I gulped at the thoughts running through my head.

Hell yeah, you make me greedy. What I ended up saying was, "I'm not the one who started this."

"So, what you're saying is since I started this, I should be the one to finish it?" His voice dripped innuendo. If this was some type of fever dream or one-off, I couldn't let it end yet. Not until I saw it all the way through. Got to live out my fantasy of Camp returning my feelings and claiming my body the same way he'd claimed my heart so long ago.

Choking on a reply, I simply nodded. Actions spoke louder than words, after all. With that adage in my head, I opened my knees wider and lifted my legs to hook them around his torso again. His nostrils flared before he closed the distance between our faces.

Anticipating another all-consuming kiss, my eyelids fluttered shut. I waited with bated breath for him to blur the lines of our delicate friendship. Everything melted away when I felt the weight of his forehead rest against my own. The new and unexpected connection made me feel safe and warm in his embrace. Cherished. His breaths ghosted across my heated flesh, he was right there.

"Camp?" My eyelids fluttered back open to take it all in. To confirm that I wasn't bugging and this was really happening.

"Tell me you want this." *Tell me you want me,* I heard the underlying meaning behind his order deep in my chest. As if he channeled some of the same insecurities as me, and it almost gutted me. My acting abilities must've been topnotch if this man never got one whiff of my crush on him. All throughout high school it remained an open secret between me and Candy. She even teased me about it countless times, but I usually nipped it in the bud the moment Camp came around.

Maybe, just maybe, she'd kept it to herself all these years. *God bless the woman and her loyalty.* But it did me no favors this time around with his deep gaze on mine. Requesting permission for entry into the deepest parts of my soul. Almost as if he wanted front-row seats to the inner workings of me.

After hiding this decade-long crush behind a smart mouth and flashes of annoyance that were mostly fake, I wasn't sure how to adequately communicate all the things rolling inside my head. There were not enough words or time in the day to share my heart's desire, but dammit if I wouldn't give it a shot. Seeing this night through was as much for me as it was for him.

In answer, I lifted both of my hands to his face. His prickly stubble tickled the sensitive skin of my palms. I craved another kiss, whether it was owed to me or not. Still, the matter of his directive remained. Even though it wasn't a question, it required a response. Something that wouldn't get misinterpreted or kill the mood.

Because there was no way I planned to wake up from this dream come true until I was good and ready.

"You said that you would've claimed me back in high school, but what if I told you...I would've let you." I whispered the last part like some kind of confession, zipping my mouth shut right after to let the truth sink in for him.

It only took a few seconds for a deep groan to sound. My body trembled at the way his large hands clutched the sides of my thighs.

"Fuck me, Zinn." The visuals alone were enough to do me in. Flames flickered to life in the dark pools of his irises, and I wanted us naked and writhing beneath the sheets as quickly as possible.

"I'm really hoping to."

"Ugh, this mouth of yours. Always sends me to the fucking edge."

"Does it?" I asked demurely, smiling. My cheeks quivered with how nervous and giddy he made me.

"Once we cross this line, Zinn, there's no going back. You're mine and I'm yours." His firm grip on me fell away as he smacked his palms against the countertop of the kitchen island. "Dammit, I wanted to give you a little more time to get used to me again, but after tonight I doubt I can wait."

"Then don't." Granting him permission felt like a no-brainer. Easily one of the best decisions I've made in a good, long while. "Waiting's overrated anyway."

"You're so right."

Camp's smirk hypnotized me. Next thing I knew, he shoved his hands between the counter and my bottom, cupped the globes of my ass cheeks again, and then we were moving. A surprised sound left my mouth as I wrapped my arms around his neck and my legs more securely around his torso.

He marched us down the hall. A look of pure determination and hunger clouded his eyes. The air snapped, crackled, and popped. I wanted his energy directed at me for as long as possible. All night. *I mean, forever makes me sound greedy, but who cares?*

I was squarely in the 'starting over' era of my life, why not dream big and manifest some shit? Become my boldest self for a change? After the last few months of life imploding, I gave myself permission to let loose. Chuck deuces at caution and common sense for a while to see where the night inevitably led us.

The chemistry was chemistrying, lighting me up from the inside out. Even as he kicked a door open and laid me down on a bed, I still felt like we floated on this wave full of lust and long-held desires. A bottleneck waiting to erupt. Our anger had been all but snuffed out and replaced with a cluster of emotions that now seemed too difficult to curtail or outright ignore.

His dark gaze ravished me as he straightened to his full height again, not taking his eyes off me.

"Camp, what are you doing?"

"Committing the image of my dream girl spread out on my mattress to memory," he stated in the most matter-of-fact way.

"And why's that? Think I'm gonna run or something?"

"If you run I'll just chase after you this time."

Holding my breath after his unexpected statement for seconds too long had the air rushing out of me. It was the resolute promise in his deepening tone that got my heart flying. It worked its way through my system, tunneling to the deepest and darkest parts of my soul where negativity and disbelief still lingered. His words and the heat of his stare chipped away at me until thoughts of our likely incompatibility vanished into thin air.

I couldn't deny the crackling heat. Or the fact that my body called to him in new and exciting ways.

I squirmed under his watchful gaze, rubbing my thighs raw to temper the flood of lust and need slamming into me.

He moved then. Almost in slow-motion. My eyes cataloged every tick and twitch of his jaw as he closed the distance between us. He was a predator while I was his helplessly willing prey, waiting to be caught and devoured. Hell, it felt like I'd been holding my breath for an eternity at this point.

"Campbell, quit stalling already."

"Impatient one, I see."

Sucking my teeth, I gave him my best stank eye. And the evil man actually chuckled. The deep, joyful sound worked its way through me. From the roots of my hair to the tips of my toes until I couldn't help but join in his mirth.

Who am I kidding? Even when he got on my damned nerves, I loved being in his vicinity. His orbit was so magnetic that it became downright impossible to resist or stay mad at him.

"This makes me sound like some sort of masochist, but I love it when you turn that attitude on me."

"Why?" My head tilted in disbelief. I had to hear his answer right this second.

"Cause it means your focus is on me." Our gazes stayed locked on each other, neither of us looking away. He seemed infinitely closer even though we weren't skin to skin the way I wanted.

"You're serious?"

"More than, Zinn. I didn't know how much I was starving until I got my first taste of you."

"Now that you know, what are you gonna do about it?" *What the hell are you waiting for then?*

"Okay, my greedy girl. I'm reading your message loud and clear."

"Well, read faster, dammit."

That deep chuckle sounded again, and a tremor rocked through me. Like the precursor to a big earthquake. One that I wasn't sure I had truly prepared for, but fear wouldn't stop me. Not now that we were here. Finally. *Fucking finally,* I thought as he draped his tall, wide frame over my smaller one.

And maybe I had turned greedy because as soon as he was close enough, I wrapped my arms around his neck and clung to him. With next-level urgency taking over, my fingers slid across his scalp and carded through short but full locks of hair.

I watched his eyelids shutter and then a rumble came from somewhere inside him.

"You sure know how to get under my skin."

Making sure to drive him further up the wall, I rolled my hips and spread my thighs wider in undeniable invitation.

"Fuck. Okay." Camp bent his head and laid a quick kiss on my lips. I followed him as he put inches between us again.

"Okay," he repeated. "I think we should get naked now."

I would've cackled at the flustered but determined way he delivered that line if I wasn't so hard up myself.

"About damned time" was what I managed to say as I shoved at his shoulders.

Because a girl needed enough room to strip.

Chapter Eleven

Zinn practically begged me to ravish her. With her gaze and those mouthy challenges. She wanted me to devour her. Fuck her into the mattress the way I'd dreamt about more than a dozen times. *Six ways from Sunday.*

So, who was I to deny my girl? Shit, I was the man who wanted to promise her the world. I planned to make her happiness my business. High up there with my other priorities. *Whatever it takes.*

Her body vibrated beneath mine, dragging me under its spell like a siren's call. I wanted to elevate the anticipation a bit more. Make sure the both of us were crazy with need, but dammit if I didn't think we were already past that point of no return. I had Zinn spread out for me on the mattress like a bona fide feast.

Every single teenage fantasy paled in comparison to this vision. This reality. When she shoved at my shoulders to create some breathing room the air stalled in my chest. Then, I nearly swallowed my tongue the second I realized she did it only to take off her clothes. It was a sight to behold. Her dark-brown skin flushed. Her pupils dilated. Zinn's chest rose and fell rapidly as if she couldn't quite catch her breath.

The buttons of the shirtdress she wore caused some issues. Seeing her struggling got my brain to react. After yanking off the first layer of my flannel shirt, I moved in to help. My own fingers fumbled around awkwardly with two buttons. The dewier skin I revealed, the more my dick took notice, distracting my good intentions.

"Fuck this," I grunted, my patience suddenly evaporating. My hands got a mind of their own as they framed her curves while gliding down her sides. Stopping at the bottom of the dress, right where it bunched up at her thighs, I grabbed the thin jean fabric in my fists and reversed my path upward.

She wiggled and lifted various body parts to help my efforts. The mission to get her naked became a joint endeavor now. Every inch of skin I uncovered felt like a revelation. A gift from heaven. Once her lower half was completely revealed to me, I could no longer resist the temptation in my midst.

Licking dry lips, I lowered myself down and laid kisses along her beautiful stretch of skin, starting with her tummy. Zinn trembled beneath me, expelling the prettiest sounds that had my balls aching and my still-covered cock stiffening.

Her hands found their way to my head again. The pads of her fingers scratching against my scalp and sending an electric current through my body. She had me hook, line, and sinker. There was no going back after this. No tenuous friendship. No ceasefire. Zinn would be mine and mine alone from this day forward.

Soon as I pushed her clothes over her breasts my movements faltered for a split second. I memorized the sexy image of her matching bra and panty set. The dark grape against her skin tone played havoc on my composure. Hell, I wanted to lay claim to her right then and there. Thrust into her tight body, watch as she accepts me, and then never ever leave.

Fuck, we hadn't even gotten to that point, yet my mind was already there. In the trenches. I gave the globes of her breasts open mouth kisses, tonguing and nipping the flesh until Zinn pressed up against me.

"We're almost there, baby. Lift up." A half-lidded gaze met mine as I raised up to finish the task at hand. Her thick tresses fanned over the comforter as she laid her head against the mattress again.

I couldn't get enough of the sexy image in front of me. Zinn wore only her bra and panties. Her hair unraveled, appearing wild and free. Chest rising and falling in rapid succession as her body squirmed from my attention. The air in the room vibrated around us, further adding to the urgency pumping through my veins. Her slightly round tummy called to me again, but I resisted for the moment. I needed something else from her first.

"Take off your bra and panties, Zinn." My voice came out dark and sinister. I gulped after issuing the command, waiting and watching as seconds ticked by.

Her eyes widened and then returned to their half-lidded state. When she finally moved, it felt like I could breathe normally again.

It took a moment to figure out that she started with the bra. Before I got my first, real look at her full breasts, she paused all movement.

Looking me dead in the eyes, she issued her own soft challenge. "You, too, Camp. I want to see you. Touch you."

"Hell yeah!" I said, body immediately moving into action by whipping off my undershirt before tackling the button and zipper of my jeans. By the time the pants and boxer briefs were around my knees, Zinn took care of the last remaining item. Using her elbows and knees, she arched her back and ass up and pushed the slip of fabric down. I watched the path with extreme interest, cataloging everything about this woman including the purple polish on her toenails.

I was naked and hard, my cock pointing toward my belly button and a trail of precum leaking from my tip. No longer able to ignore it, I wrapped a fist around the shaft and stroked myself. Starting at her pretty toes, my gaze inched up her body, taking the scenic route. I wouldn't dare miss a single sight or sound from her.

Somehow, I knew we'd get here eventually. Despite our rocky association in high school, it was damn near love at first sight for me back then. And over the years, I'd nurtured this need and desire for her until it blossomed, growing into a desperate and possessive urgency to claim. Thankfully, Zinn didn't seem to mind that we were skipping a few steps. Her enthusiasm torpedoed the last bit of anger from tonight's outing. At the same time, it also knocked down any remaining hesitancy.

She craved this just as much as I did.

I set my gaze on her face once more and instantly noticed where her focus lingered now. On me leisurely fisting my cock. A knowing smile pulled at my lips. Whether she realized it or not, her legs opened wider in unspoken invitation. *Damn, that's sexy as hell.*

"You want me inside you, Zinn?"

She blinked pretty brown eyes up at me. "Yes, I need you."

"Not before I have another taste." My dick could wait a little while longer. I was desperate for a different kind of kiss. The kind that would have her rocking against my mouth and leaving her essence imprinted on my tongue. I wanted her body ready to accept me when I entered her for the very first time.

Without wasting a second on useless words, I got on my knees, grabbed her spread thighs, and jerked her body until the space between us disappeared.

Zinn's scent filled my nostrils. Short, coarse pubic hair covered her mound. I traced the seam of her cunt with the pad of my thumb, teasing her. And myself. Her thighs quaked in my strong hold.

"Camp..." Zinn's breath hitched on my name. "Please." Her plea sent a lightning bolt through me, igniting the fire between us into a raging blaze.

"I got you, baby."

Putting us both out of our miseries, I dove in tongue-first and nearly shot my load; her taste was just that explosive. Addictive. I became a man stranded in the desert who luckily found a water source right in the nick of time. And fuck me if I wasn't dehydrated.

"Mmph." I groaned into her pussy, finding and latching onto her clitoris after tonguing her slick folds. She rolled her hips and fisted my hair to keep me close as she worked herself on my tongue, taking what she needed. What I would never fucking deny her. There was nowhere else I'd rather be than right here giving her pleasure.

"Oh," she gasped the most perfect sound when I flicked her clit then sucked. Her cream coated my chin just like I imagined. Still, I needed more. I wanted her beyond satisfied and completely spent from my brand of loving.

Slipping a finger between her folds, I entered her snug warmth for the first time.

"Fuck, you're so tight for me." My head spun. Her walls sucked the intruding digit in, squeezing around it so damn tightly that I knew my dick would have a helluva time lasting long. She already felt like heaven and hell. Sweet and spicy. I could bury myself inside her all the time and never want for anything or anyone else.

"Ungh. Right there." I worked a second finger inside, diving back in to flick and nip at her swollen bud, intent on driving her over the edge.

More moans and gasps hit the air as I fucked my fingers into her wet cunt. Her juices coated my digits and chin. Fuck if this wasn't even better than whatever my imagination cooked up. The only thing that would make it perfect would be her orgasm. A sweet and wanton release at my hands. Something told me she wasn't far from reaching it.

"Camp, more!" She begged. *Her wish is my command,* I thought. I'd move heaven and earth to give her what she wanted. Needed. Anything and everything she desired. Except running away from me.

I doubled my efforts, delivering short and fast pumps while sucking at her clit. The perfect storm brewed between our bodies. Her rolling hips jerked. A harsh tremor started in Zinn's thighs.

"I'm..." she shrieked right as her folds fluttered around my fingers before squeezing it in a vise grip. Then, she shattered against me. Her body froze for a moment. All of a sudden, the dam broke, and she was cumming. And it was the most glorious feeling. Her fingers gripped and pulled at my skull as she held me close.

It felt like a lifetime had passed before the trembling subsided enough that her body slackened.

As soon as she seemed to melt back into the mattress, I got my first look at a completely debauched Zinn. It was a sight I wouldn't likely forget for the rest of my life.

In a state of euphoria, she barely noticed my movement.

Quickly snagging and donning a condom, I returned to the position between her thick thighs, ready to claim my dream girl once and for all.

"Open your eyes and look at me, beautiful."

With the cutest smile on her lips, she exhaled, and long lashes fluttered open for me.

Poised and ready, I nudged the head of my cock at her entrance, needing her full and undivided attention.

She wrapped her legs around my hips and urged me undeniably forward.

"You're mine now, Zinn."

"I know. How about you make it official?" Her hooded gaze cast a spell on me, demanding I make us one. So, that's exactly what I did. With Zinn's eyes on me and her fingers carding through my hair, I entered her body with one single thrust. Bottoming out, I waited for her to adjust to the intrusion and welcome me like I desperately needed her to.

I groaned at the way her walls pulsed around my shaft. "Move, Camp. Please."

Denying her wasn't in my DNA. I retreated only to sink back into her heavenly warmth, setting a pace and rhythm meant to catapult us to the finish line. This first time would be fast and furious. No doubt about it. Hell, it was even beyond my control at this point. My cock and balls had a mind of their own, driven mad by the sensations and feelings of home she evoked. Every molecule in my body had been on the exact same page since the beginning.

I switched up my strokes between fast and hard to long and slow, trying every trick in the book to hold off the inevitable explosion.

We needed to reach Nirvana together. My pride would accept nothing less. Pulling out, her tortured moan fed my ego like nothing else. I shifted our bodies so that we were on our sides, her back plastered against my chest. Grabbing Zinn's left thigh, I spread her open for me and entered her again. Her body pulled me in deeper at this angle, and I loved it.

"God, Camp, you're so deep."

Fucking her sideways like this would become one of my favorite positions. Remembering why I moved us in the first place, my hand glided across her dewy skin until reaching its ultimate goal. I covered her mound, inching towards where we were joined together. I couldn't get enough of seeing us like this. Years of countless dreams finally fulfilled. The pads of my fingers brushed against her clit, eliciting more sounds from her. But it was a double-edged sword because I knew there was no way I could hold out much longer.

My heavy balls slapped against her cheeks with each thrust. My cock stiff as a board. I was eager to cum. Release inside my girl while she milked me dry.

I focused on her pleasure and mine. Finding that bundle of nerves again, I circled her clit and fucked into her with one goal in mind.

"Oh God, right there." Her whimpers filled my ears, surrounding me in this deep trance. I was lost to everything but her and this moment.

"Cum for me, Zinn." I held on for as long as possible and then felt the rush. The flutter of her folds started right as the first jet of cum shot into the condom.

"Fuck, baby." Zinn pulsed around my jerking shaft, extending my orgasm to new heights. I burrowed my face between her neck and shoulder, sucking on the skin there. Marking her in another way. Strands of her hair plastered to my drenched face, and it didn't bother me in the slightest. I loved how intimate this all felt. How different our relationship would be from now on. My softening cock jerked inside her at the mere thought of her leaving marks on me too.

Yeah, this is only the beginning for us.

"Mmm." She muttered sleepily, snuggling her body closer to mine. Now that the anger had been fucked out of us and our hunger temporarily sated, I'd let her get some rest. But I knew full well there would be a second and third round before the sun came up.

Chapter Twelve

The weekend passed in this hazy blur full of sex and cuddles. My face hurt from all the smiling I'd done. Even my new co-workers noticed the apparent change in my aura. A glow they said.

Two weeks later, it still felt like I floated on cloud nine.

Camp and I had easily settled into domestic bliss. We talked and laughed together, getting to know one another on a much deeper, more personal level. Of course, we'd been familiar with each other for half our lives at this point, but nothing compared to the new intimacy building between us. It was real. Better than anything I imagined in past fantasies. Or whenever my thoughts turned to Camp and what my life might've looked like if we stopped our petty bickering as teens.

It all felt a little too easy, though. The tiniest pessimistic voice in my head still wondered when the other shoe might drop. When the rose-colored glasses cleared up, and we reverted back to our old, childish behaviors.

Once Friday rolled around and my shortened workday ended, my phone vibrated with a notification. I pulled the device out of my front pocket for a quick peek at the locked screen. Seeing Candy's name, I unlocked the phone and clicked on the message preview.

> I'm baaaack! We're finally in the same zip code again.

Before I wiggled my fingers to type a response, she'd already beat me to it with another message.

> When can I see your face? I miss you, bestie.

> I get off work in an hour. Want to meet at your place?

> YES. I'll have wine and snacks ready!

> LOL. Ofc you better. See you soon.

> We have a lot to catch up on...

The happy grin splitting my face at our rapid-fire text exchange nearly fell at Candy's last message. *Does she know?* I wondered to myself. But how could she know about this new development when I still wasn't sure how my relationship with Camp had changed so much in a short time span.

Is she okay with it? Or does she hate the idea of us together? She'd teased me mercilessly in high school after figuring out my secret. It was one thing to know about my crush on her twin brother and another to learn that we're now smashing.

A student approaching the Services Desk put a halt to my spiraling thoughts. Once I clocked out and was in my car headed to the address Candy sent, I realized there was no escaping my best friend and the way she pulled information out of me. Only time would tell if she was happy or livid about me and Camp.

Thankful that she said there'd be wine, I readied myself for either option.

My social calendar blossomed in a matter of weeks. Between Camp, Thursday evenings with the Plucking Ladies Garden Club and the occasional weekend soirée, and now my bestie calling me to hang out, it felt like I was on the move nonstop. And I wouldn't change a thing. I was pretty damned surprised how everything seemed to come together for me after crawling back home. *Who knew!*

I found a prime parking spot across the street from her apartment building and sat in the idling car to gather my thoughts.

Belatedly, it crossed my mind to send Camp a message and tell him about the change in plans for today.

Warmth flushed my skin at the sweet offer and his use of "home." Camp's kindness shouldn't surprise me, but it sure made my knees feel like jelly. Hell, they would've been knocking together if I were standing.

Shutting my eyes, I gave myself a twenty-second pep talk, cut the ignition off, and then opened the driver-side door.

Candy buzzed me in not even a beat after I pressed the button for her apartment number. I would've chuckled at her eagerness if my stomach wasn't tied in knots.

Stalling was no longer an option. As soon as I shuffled off the elevator, my best friend in the whole wide world waited for me at the threshold of her apartment door.

A smile split my face as the worries faded into the background. Although we've stayed in contact through messages, calls, and the occasional video chat, nothing felt quite like seeing each other in person. And it'd been actual years. When I moved to California, neither one of our schedules seemed to gel well. Especially since getting down to Los Angeles from the Central Coast wasn't always quick or easy.

"You're really here!" Candy yelled. I quickened my steps and made it to her in moments. We hugged for a long time at her door, both of us emotional.

"Come in," she said once we pulled apart. "I've got all the wine. We need to catch up now!"

"Okay." I stepped over the threshold into Candy's pristine apartment and took off my pointed-toe flats after noticing the light-colored carpet.

"Don't worry about that." I ignored the way she waved a dismissive hand at my actions. Hell, this was almost as much about getting comfortable as it was about being considerate.

"Red or white?" Candy called from somewhere around the corner after rushing off.

"I'm not picky. You choose," I responded as I walked down the short hallway and turned left into the open-concept kitchen. This time of day, sunlight brightened the space. It felt light and airy, exactly like the vibes my best friend gave off.

"Let's start with white then. I brought a few bottles home from Europe."

"You sure you don't want to wait and open them for a special occasion?"

"Having my best friend back in town is special enough. It's the perfect occasion, if you ask me."

I smiled, not bothering to argue with her.

She filled two wine glasses almost to the brim and gestured at the tray of snacks on the counter. "Will you grab the snacks? I'll handle the booze."

"Sure thing."

Candy took our glasses and the bottle to the living room, placing the items on the round, glass coffee table.

"Your place is really nice, Candy."

"Thanks. My parents and Camp helped me with it. First, I thought about buying a house, but I'm gone too much. It would be a waste."

"There's still time. We are only twenty-five, ya know. I swear you and your brother are overachievers."

"Speaking of my brother…"

I put my hand up. "Let me stop you right there. Can I at least take a sip of my wine first?"

My best friend sighed the most dramatic, put-upon sigh I've ever heard or witnessed in my life. "Go ahead."

"Thank you." I grabbed a glass and thought seriously about chugging it. But I knew that wouldn't solve a damned thing or stop the upcoming interrogation headed my way. Instead, I took a healthy sip of the delicious wine then pulled my legs up and rested against the sofa cushion. My nerves were frayed, but there was little to be done about it now.

"All good?" Unsure if she asked about the wine or me, I played dumb.

"It's delicious, thanks."

Candy took a sip from her own glass, turned her body towards mine, and raised a manicured brow in question.

"So, you and Camp, huh?"

"I'm not sure what you mean…" I stalled.

"Don't play that game with me, Zinnia Whitfield. Plus, my brother sent me a text sharing the news earlier this week."

"He did what?!" Thankful that I hadn't taken another sip, I sputtered in shock.

"Camp was all too happy to let me know that he'd finally won you over. I could feel my twin's glee through the message." She shook her head.

Won me over? What the hell? *She can't be saying what I think she's saying. Can she?*

"Camp has been head over heels for you since high school, Zinn."

"You have got to be fucking with me." Frozen in place, I stared at the woman across from me. For several moments, it felt like I couldn't move. Couldn't breathe. I was speechless.

"I'm afraid not, bestie. My brother is down bad. Has been since high school." With both hands holding the bowl of her glass, Candy took another sip of her wine like it was the best tea in the world.

"But we used to throw barbs at each other like we were sworn enemies. He couldn't have felt the same way as me." I refused to believe it.

Nothing she said made a lick of sense. It was something the younger version of me had always held out hope for…in the furthest recesses of my mind. Every person wanted their crush to return their feelings on some level. And since I assumed we'd annoyed each other too much to ever get along, I stored my hopes away for safekeeping.

As soon as college applications rolled around, I became hellbent on leaving the state for new experiences. Getting accepted to a school right next to the beach had me packing and moving before summer vacation even came to a close. I'd wanted a fresh start. A new beginning.

Still, none of that meant I'd left my life back in Dallas buried. Just like I hadn't left thoughts of Camp behind. No matter how hard I tried.

Candy had shared consistent updates so much that I was able to keep up with Camp's life despite the distance. The slightest good news about him lit a fire within my heart. In turn, I'd pushed myself hard to make it at school and in California. Things were going well enough until I couldn't accept being passed over again and again at work. It was disheartening, to say the least.

"Well don't leave me in suspense." Candy cut through the maze of my thoughts. "How's it been going since y'all got together?"

"It's been surreal, actually."

"Surreal, huh? How so?" Gazing at me, she took another sip from her wine glass while mine almost sat forgotten in the space between my crossed legs.

"I'm pretty sure you're well aware of the type of guy your brother is."

"I am," she nodded with an all-knowing grin.

"He took me in without batting an eyelash all those weeks ago. I can't even imagine where I'd be right now if I hadn't worked up the nerve to call him. Or if he didn't pick up."

"Oh, Zinn. There was no chance in hell my brother would ever leave you stranded. He'd gladly been on standby for you. Now and when we were younger."

"Knowing Camp, he would've done the same for anybody."

"Uh-uh, that's where you're wrong, sis. I mean, my brother is a stand-up guy and an amazing friend. Don't get me wrong. He's one in a million. But he was not about to drop everything to move just anybody into his house without a second thought. That's his sanctuary, Zinn."

His sanctuary.

"You mean to tell me I'm special or something?" I tried to play it off as some joke while my head continued to spin. Seeking a temporary distraction, I lifted the glass to my lips and took another sip.

"That's exactly what I'm saying, and you damn well know it."

"Alright, alright. Can we change the subject, please? At least for a bit." I pleaded. Batting my eyelashes with the saddest pout I could muster was peak behavior, and it worked like magic.

"I guess I'll allow it. But don't think we won't circle back around to this topic again. Drink up," she gestured at my glass. "There's more where that came from."

It didn't take much encouragement from her to finish off my wine after that whirlwind conversation had my stomach in knots. "So, how was Europe?"

"Amazing," she sighed wistfully. I got the impression that although Candy traveled nonstop due to her job as a flight attendant, it wasn't often she got to spend time simply being a tourist.

The pictures she posted on social media told their own story, but her smile was the brightest I'd ever seen it.

She caught me up on her trip, sharing details about the weekend she was able to meet up with her parents. We ate snacks and drank our weights in wine while giggling and talking our way through the late afternoon. By the time the sun set, I was well and truly tipsy. So, when Candy went to the bathroom, I pulled out my phone and shot off a text to Camp.

Hey, handsome. Pls come get me in 2hrs

No prob, beautiful. See you soon!

I grinned from ear to ear as Candy stumbled back into the living room. "I ordered food," she announced. "It should be here in thirty minutes."

"Perfect." Wine tended to sneak up on me like it did now. I needed something more substantial than the light snacks Candy had set out for us that were nearly gone.

"Camp's coming to get me in two hours," I told her.

"Oh, is he now?"

"Quit teasing me already, Candy." There was no telling when I'd be ready to circle back to our conversation about her brother, but it still didn't feel like the best time. I refused to jinx anything related to Camp. Everything had been going exceedingly well in the past two weeks; it felt like a dream. And too good to be true.

"I'll let it slide for now. But I can't promise about the next time."

Candy struggled to open another bottle of wine while I watched unhelpfully. In all honesty, I would just get in her way if I did offer my help. Once she eased the cork off with a shout of triumph, I grabbed our empty glasses from the coffee table and held them up as she poured.

What's the harm in having a few more glasses? The food would soak up a lot of this liquid sloshing around in my stomach, I reasoned.

I'd come to find out that splitting one bottle of wine with my bestie was already past my limit.

Lesson plucking learned, indeed.

Chapter Thirteen

At half past seven, I booked a ride and waited ten minutes for it to arrive. Something told me Zinn wouldn't be sober enough to drive back home, so that left the task up to me. And I was more than happy to scoop my girl up. Her text came through right as I walked through my front door after spending a few hours on my latest project. The paperwork had been signed, and I received the keys which meant that I dove right into planning and project manager mode.

I compiled pages and pages of small and large tasks that should keep me busy over the next few months at least.

Heavy traffic seemed unavoidable on a Friday night. I sat back, peered out the window, and watched the scenery go by. Neither me nor the driver had much to say during the ride, which I was low-key thankful for. A conversation would've just been a distraction from my thoughts about Zinn.

I wondered about the scene I'd find at Candy's condo. When my sister got together with her bestie, anything was possible. They both had a lot to catch up on. We'd been close since the days in the womb, and nothing much got past my sister. She'd stayed in my business as much as I allowed, whether I liked it or not. Nowadays, I made fewer attempts to hide things from her. It was less hassle and headache in the long run.

Knowing that Candy headed back home from her European trip, I pre-emptively sent her message announcing our status change. For me, it only made sense that she was the first to know given how important Candy was in both our lives. Plus, my twin sister wouldn't let me hear the end of it if it'd gone any other way.

And she'd be the first person in line to kick my ass if I hurt Zinn. *Which is never gonna happen.* Now that she's my girl, there's no chance of going back to the days of childish animosity. We were beyond that now.

My new purpose was to build a life with and for her. After only a week, Zinn likely had no idea about the severity of my feelings, but she soon would. I refused to spook her, though. Especially if we weren't on the same page quite yet. Still, it felt like we were almost there, just a page or two behind one another at this point. I'd keep plucking away. Treating her like the queen she's always been in my heart.

Finally, the driver slowed on Candy's block. As soon as the car came to a stop, I thanked the man, got out, and took a moment on the curb to add a tip in the app. Looking around my sister's quiet neighborhood, my gaze landed on Zinn's dark sedan across the street. A wave of relief slapped me mid-chest.

Although I hated to break up their best friend session, the need to lay eyes on my girl pressed me forward like never before. Hell, this was the longest we'd been apart since she moved back home and in with me. When her text came through hours ago, I knew there was no hope left for me. Or her. Zinn asking me to scoop her up from my sister's place made me feel like I'd won the damn lottery. She could depend on me for anything. Big or small. She could put her trust in me without worry or second guesses. Because, as her man, there wasn't a thing I wouldn't do for her.

I buzzed myself in at the downstairs entrance. Just like Candy kept a key to my home, I had one for her place in case of emergency.

Seeing an old lady struggling with a cart while entering behind me, I stopped to offer my help. We rode the elevator together, and I made sure she arrived at her apartment. Then, I was back on mission to get Zinn. There was no telling what the two women had gotten up to for hours, and the curiosity added an extra bounce to my step as I exited the elevator on Candy's floor and strode to her apartment. Quietly listening at the door, straining my ears, I finally heard a round of giggles. In that moment, gratitude settled over me. Behind this door were two of the most important women in my life, and they were happy and enjoying their time together. I hated interrupting, but nothing would stop me from doing so. I'd stalled as much as possible.

Knock. Knock. Knock. My knuckles thumped against Candy's front door. Seconds later, the cheerful laughter died down, and I heard soft footsteps nearing my position.

"Who is it?" Thankful that my sister still knew to check even though she'd been drinking, my shoulders relaxed a smidge. My protective instincts were always activated around these two. And I refused to apologize or change my ways.

"It's me, sis." A handful of seconds ticked by before the telltale sounds of locks disengaging reached my ears.

"Hey, big bro!" I smiled down at my twin sister who appeared tipsy. "Why didn't you use your key?" she asked while spinning around and marching back down the hallway. Towards Zinn if I had to guess. I secured the door behind me and followed.

"That's for emergencies, Can. You want me just willy-nilly entering your condo?"

She stopped abruptly before reaching the end of the short hallway. "You make an excellent point. Thanks for respecting my space." She hiccupped at the end.

Oh boy!

"Of course, Can." I shook my head. Seeing the state Candy was in, the thought of pushing past her to lay eyes on my girl came to mind, but I resisted the urge.

"Zinn's waiting for you." She tossed me a know-it-all glance over her shoulder then started moving again.

Suddenly, it felt like my feet had wings because I couldn't get to her fast enough. Once we cleared the hallway, I got my first look at my girlfriend, happily munching on something as she lounged on the couch.

A sight for sore eyes, she is and will forever be. Amen.

When her head tilted up and her gaze met mine, those pretty brown eyes lit the fuck up. My cock twitched, but I slammed the door shut on the sudden need flooding my system. Getting a boner with my sister in the room felt all kinds of wrong.

"Hey, baby."

Zinn blinked and then shook her head adorably, as if she had to clear it.

"Okay, sir. I'mma need you to turn that rizz all the way down," she said, pointing a finger at me with mild accusation and one eye squinting.

"I have no idea what rizz you speak of." A smile pulled at my lips, cheeks twitching with mirth. Drunk Zinn was a riot and a half. Something told me I'd have my hands full tonight, and the thought only made me more excited to get her home.

"Don't play coy with me, Campbell Matheson. I've got your number."

Meanwhile, Candy stood off to the side, taking in the show we were inadvertently putting on. I wondered what went through my sister's head but didn't have the balls to really ask out loud. With the two empty wine bottles sitting on the coffee table, her filter probably took a vacation for the rest of the night. There was absolutely no point inviting trouble right now.

"You ready to head out, Zinn?" I took in the mini tornado that was Candy's living room. Food containers littered the coffee table, along with the empty bottles and wine glasses. From all appearances, it seemed like the girls had a fun time catching up.

"Yeah, I think so." I watched her careful attempt to stand and had to swallow a chuckle.

When she noticed how quiet the room got, she looked up. "Uh, maybe I'll use the bathroom first."

"Okay."

As soon as Zinn escaped the living room, Candy spun around and got all up in my face.

"Spill. The. Tea." She punctuated each word with a pointy finger to my chest.

I arched my brow to stall for time. Candy was too smart for that, despite her inebriated state.

"Give me something, bro. Zinn has been so damned tight-lipped the entire day; I could barely get anything out of her. I think she's scared."

Scared. "Of me?" I asked, my heart in my throat all of a sudden.

Candy scrunched up her face. "Not necessarily. Maybe she thinks your newfound relationship isn't real. That it's all temporary."

"It's not," I stated adamantly.

"You and I know this." She waved her hand between us and continued, "but Zinn hasn't gotten there quite yet for whatever reason."

Even though I'd already arrived at similar thinking, I listened to what my sister had to say. If she'd sensed that much from Zinn without her sharing much of anything then it might be worse than I initially feared.

Shifting the timeline—yet again—seemed to be in order. Since there was no skin off my back, I'd double my efforts to set Zinn's mind at ease when it came to our relationship status.

She was my forever, and it was time for us to be on the same page. Because the future I envisioned for us depended on it.

"I'll handle it," I promised Candy. "You don't have to worry about her. And thanks for telling me."

She shook her head. "I wanna see you both happy. I've always considered Zinn as family. Y'all's relationship just makes it official official."

I stopped hiding my feelings for Zinn a couple of years ago from my sister. When Candy called to tell me she was finally relocating back home, I'd made my intentions clear from the jump. For one, I wanted to announce my goal to win over Zinn. And two, I had to make sure my sister had my back if necessary. This was her best friend we were talking about. If she didn't approve of our relationship then that would've been another obstacle for us. And overcoming the head-butting we'd gotten into as teens was already enough of a hurdle to begin with.

Sounds from the bathroom filtered down the hallway. When I heard the door open, Zinn appeared a few seconds later. A soft, shy smile graced her full lips.

Fuck, I'm in trouble.

"I'm ready for real this time."

Zinn went to give Candy a hug. As the two women embraced, I took several steps back to give them some privacy. My sister whispered something for her ears only, and Zinn's audible gasp piqued my curiosity again.

"Candy!" She reared back, looking scandalized. If my girl were wearing pearls right now, she'd be clutching them.

"You heard me." My sister doubled down on whatever outrageous thing she said while wearing a knowing smirk on her flushed face. "Don't act all demure with me. We're all adults now."

"Here, here," I chimed in. Zinn snapped her neck in my direction and gave me side-eye which I promptly shrugged at.

"Your turn, big bro." Candy beckoned me over with her arms spread wide. Shaking my head at her tipsy antics, I strode over and bent down to embrace her.

"Don't fuck this up, Camp."

"I wouldn't dream of it," I whispered back.

"Good. I'm counting on you to keep my bestie here and happy."

"That's definitely the plan, sis." A major part of it. Building a life with Zinn was the mission. And I planned to make it the best life possible, ensuring both our dreams come true.

"Okay," she said, dropping her arms. "I won't keep you two any longer."

"Thanks for inviting me over. I had a blast."

"Me, too. I'm still waiting to hear about the bidding results, so I'll tell you next month's schedule once I know. Hopefully, we can make this a semi-regular thing."

"Sounds good. Bye." Zinn teetered her way towards the front door. Right as she reached the knob, Candy called behind me.

"Here. She might need this." My sister passed along a bottle of water.

"Thanks. Make sure you stay hydrated, too." By the time I turned back around, Zinn had the door unlocked and was halfway over the threshold.

"Love you, sis. Take care of yourself." I called over my shoulder.

"I always do!"

Nodding, I caught up with Zinn in the hallway.

"Where's the fire?" I asked.

"Huh?" Tilting her head, she looked up at me. Whether she realized it or not, she was drunk as all hell. And fucking adorable.

"What's the hurry?" I rephrased my question.

"Oh, I wanna get home and cuddle." She pressed the button for the elevator and then aimed the sweetest, most lopsided grin at me.

"Is that right?"

"Mmhm." She nodded, and it was the most adorable fucking thing she could've done in that moment.

"Hand over your keys, baby."

"Where's your truck?" She started digging into the tote bag on her right shoulder without argument.

"It's still at the house. I got a ride over since you've been drinking."

"You're so smart." Pausing her search, she patted my chest and then went straight back to digging around in her bag for the car keys.

"Have I told you how cute you are, Zinn?"

"Nope!" She popped the 'p' loud as all get-out, and my gaze fell to her irresistible lips. "But feel free to tell me anytime." The giggle that came next went directly to my heart, promptly traveling further south. My response couldn't be helped. She had a firm chokehold on my emotions and libido.

The elevator finally arrived. Since Zinn remained distracted, I ushered her onto the lift and the second the doors slid closed she produced the keys triumphantly. As she handed them over, I thanked her. Less than five minutes after leaving my sister's condo, we made it downstairs, and I got Zinn situated in her car, buckling her seatbelt.

"Thank you, handsome."

"Anytime, sweetheart." Shutting the passenger side door, I jogged around the front of Zinn's car and claimed the driver's seat, taking a moment to adjust it for my longer frame. "How about we get you home and to bed."

"Mm, sounds perfect."

To me, too. The past several weeks had been a necessary restart for us. A destined one. And it was only the beginning.

Chapter Fourteen

With my happy little buzz going, I quickly came to the realization that I could get used to being a passenger-seat princess. Hell, it already felt like I was currently living my best life, and we'd only been in the car for a few minutes.

"Did you have fun tonight, Zinn?"

I peeked my eyes open and glanced over at Camp as he easily maneuvered my vehicle through Friday night traffic.

"I had a blast. Hanging out with Candy is just what I needed."

"Glad to hear it."

"Thank you for agreeing to pick me up. I wasn't expecting to drink quite that much, but wine tends to go straight to my head."

The sound of Camp's low chuckle slid across my skin like the softest caress. "You don't have to thank me. It's completely my pleasure."

"Your pleasure, huh?"

The car got quiet for a minute before he said, "In case you haven't figured it out yet, I'd do anything for you."

I shifted against the seat, angling my body towards him. Turning, with the side of my head on the backrest, my thoughts tumbled out my mouth as if my usual filter took a vacation. "Mm. You're tryna spoil me, Campbell Matheson. And I think I like it." *I like you. I more than like you.*

"I more than like you, too, Zinnia Whitfield."

My heart skipped, and I gasped the biggest gasp upon realizing that my final thought had leaked out somehow.

Flushing from head to toe, I couldn't say another word.

"Don't get shy on me now, Zinn."

"Who's shy? Not me." The blatant lie rolled off my tongue effortlessly. Too bad the sudden squeak in my voice gave me away.

"Yeah, okay." His deep gaze seared me before returning to the road.

"So, how was your day? Do anything fun?"

"I did, actually. Went over to the new place and started ordering a few materials. I'll begin demo next week for sure."

I'd picked his brain on several occasions now and knew he was talking about the demolition part of his latest renovation. Wrecking shit before he made it all nice and habitable again.

"Does the house need a ton of work then?"

"Nah, not really. It has good bones and nothing surprising showed up on the inspector's report. But, at the end of the day, I won't truly know until I really get in there and start tearing shit up. Right now, my list consists mostly of cosmetic changes."

"Will you give me a tour sometime?"

He glanced in my direction. "Of course. We can go tomorrow or Sunday if you want."

"Okay. Let's play the weekend by ear," I said. I had no business making plans with how much wine I consumed tonight, but Camp didn't need to know all that.

"Whatever you say, sweetheart. Just tell me what day sounds good for you."

"Mm, will do."

A comfortable silence settled over us. The combination of that and knowing I was safe with Camp lulled me. My eyelids fluttered shut without permission, and there wasn't anything I could do about it.

Plus, the only truth hovering at the forefront of my mind was that Camp would protect me with his life.

So, I stopped fighting and let myself succumb to a quick nap.

Weightless. I floated on a cloud, encased within the sturdiest and warmest cocoon ever. It was giving love and protection like I'd never experienced before. Notes of bergamot and amber wood filled the air, tickling my nostrils.

Realizing that my body was actually on the move when it shouldn't be, the last of the sleep fog faded as I fully woke up. I blinked to clear the lingering drowsiness, and there was Camp. Carrying me as if I weighed nothing.

I drank in the sight of his side profile. The stubble of his five o'clock shadow was one of the sexiest images I wouldn't mind waking up to for the rest of my days.

Ugh, he smells so good, I thought. With my eyes closed, I turned my face into his shoulder to get a better whiff of his cologne and maybe a hint of his natural scent hidden beneath.

"I'm glad you think so." His low rumbled words skated across my flesh, making my toes tingle.

"You read minds now or something?" My voice sounded raspy and lower than usual.

"I wouldn't mind that particular superpower when it came to you, but unfortunately no. You spoke your last thought out loud, sweetheart."

"I did not." I rebuked him and his lie outright, denying his claim.

"You did," he mocked, and I tried my damnedest to burrow a hole through the same shoulder I low-key molested a second ago.

"Oh God." Apparently I wasn't awake enough yet for my brain and mouth to function properly. I felt and heard his chuckle since he held me so tightly. "You can put me down now." With his hands full of me, I had no idea how the hell he managed to get us inside the house, but now he paused in the center of the living room. The glow of the muted TV was our only light source in the quiet house.

"I like holding you."

"That's all well and good to know, but I'm not light enough for you to be carrying me all over the place. You could've woken me up, Camp."

"I certainly could have but quite enjoyed bringing you inside this way instead."

"Okay, Romeo." I rolled my eyes at him even though I swooned, as giddy as someone half my age after seeing her crush up close and personal for the first time. "Unhand me, kind sir." Fake outrage poured from my lips, but finally he followed my command. This close, though, I noted the way his eyes sparked with mirth and something more.

Unsteady on my feet for a few seconds, I clung to his wide shoulders, and he let me have my way. Figuring that my knees wouldn't betray me after a minute, I used my grip on him to lift myself up on tiptoe and laid a peck on his chin.

"Thanks for taking care of me."

Before my feet were flat on the floor again, Camp started to move, and my arms dropped as I stumbled backwards.

"What?" I stuttered. My breath hitched at the expression on his face. He reached out to wrap one arm around me. The warmth of his large palm spanned my upper back, guiding my movement and direction. He had yet to answer my question, though. A wave of need washed over me at the way his gaze devoured me as the silence stretched.

My mind cleared, the buzz from the glasses of wine earlier all but gone from my system. Camp was just that potent. The sole reason behind my skin warming and my thoughts reeling was the man in front of me. Anticipation flooded my veins. I started nipping at the inside of my mouth right at the moment the wall stopped this backward dance we engaged in, the placement of his hand softening the sudden collision.

"Camp..." I tried again.

"You never have to thank me for taking care of you, Zinn. It's what I've always done. And what I plan to continue doing." His statement rocked the foundation underneath my feet. I didn't know what to say, but my mouth worked anyway.

"I–" Camp's free hand came up to my chin, the pad of his thumb gliding across my bottom lip.

"Stop it."

Confused, I asked, "What is it?"

"You're worrying the inside of your cheeks. Stop before you hurt yourself."

This man right here is about to be the death of me, I mused. His face seemed to move closer and closer until his tall frame–his entire presence–surrounded me. Now, the only thoughts on my mind were the things he could do with that big, strong body of his. I wanted him to do every single naughty act to me this minute. Neediness took over. I was suddenly desperate for his touch, Camp's special brand of love. And I craved it now.

"Kiss me," I blurted. As if he knew exactly what ideas filled my head, he had the nerve to smile down at me. And not just any smile either. It was the devilish one chock-full of rizz. The one that had my panties sopping wet in two seconds flat and my knees knocking together no matter the time or place.

When his smile dimmed right before my eyes, I watched him gather his thoughts before speaking.

"You've been drinking, Zinn."

"So what?" I shot back.

"I don't want to take advantage of you."

I lifted my hands and grabbed the collar of his shirt, bringing our faces infinitely closer. What I had to say couldn't be misheard or misinterpreted.

"First of all, I'm not that far gone that I don't know what I'm asking you for. And secondly, there is no part of your DNA capable of taking advantage of me or anyone else. I know you, Camp." *I know you, and I love you.*

Before I fixed my mouth to further make my point, his lips pressed against mine, promptly shutting me up and fulfilling my request all in one go. I moaned when his tongue peeked out and flicked at my lips. His request for entry was obvious, and I had zero problem giving in to him.

Melting into a puddle, he pulled me closer and drank from me like I was his favorite concoction. Kissing Camp always put me in a heady space where my body flushed, my toes tingled, and I just let go and savored the moment. The experience of being present with him in such an intimate way was everything.

His hands slid down my back until he reached and grabbed handfuls of my ass cheeks, squeezing and massaging them. I mewled as our bodies instinctively brought us closer, grinding together in an age-old dance.

He broke the kiss first, giving us a brief intermission. Our breaths melded. My chest rose and fell in rapid succession; my gaze filled with him and only him. Camp's usual chestnut-brown eyes appeared almost black, darkened by his lust for me. And I wanted him to unleash that hunger of his on me. To ravish me until I was spent. Until I felt completely and utterly claimed by him.

I couldn't help the thoughts crowding my head nor did I care to try. There was only him and me here, anyway. We were all that mattered. The sparks that had flickered between us since the beginning now turned into a raging fire full of passion. Desire. *And love?*

With every fiber of my being I wanted that four-letter word to exist for us. For it to be mutual in every way imaginable. I wished on the stars that these feelings were no longer one-sided. That we had finally grown up from our antagonistic ways and moved in the direction of something better.

"I need you, Zinn." His low growl wrestled me further down the rabbit hole of need.

"Right here. Right now." Determined, I pushed at his shoulders, and he put some distance between us but not much. He didn't let go of me completely either. Once he realized I started unbuttoning my jeans and struggling out of my work blouse next, Camp got moving to help me disrobe.

"You fucking amaze me, sweetheart."

"I know. Now, you get undressed too," I ordered.

"Copy that." His hands dropped from me as he focused on his own clothes, and I couldn't even be mad at him. I wanted his hands on me without any barriers as quickly as possible. I was hungry for him. My skin flushed, the air between us sizzling. Now that we were on the same page, this rush of need hadn't escaped my notice. I found my hunger for this man growing leaps and bounds, shifting into some sort of obsession. One I was too far gone to control any longer. The genie had escaped the bottle, and there was no chance in hell I could force it back in. And with the way Camp matched my energy, I wasn't alone anymore.

Finally, I stood before him still wearing my bra and panties. In the blink of an eye, every stitch of his clothing was gone, and my body froze to take it all in. Get my fill of his finely sculpted physique. How his muscles twitched at my obvious appreciation.

"You can't look at me like that, Zinn."

"Like what?" I shot back. My smart mouth had a mind of its own when it came to him.

"Like you wanna devour me."

I licked my suddenly dry lips. His statement had me thinking of doing just that. Placing my palms flush against the walls behind me, I slowly slid down until I was on my knees in front of him. An audible gulp sounded above me, and a knowing smirk teased at my lips.

"What are you doing?" He asked, tripping over the unnecessary question.

"Exactly what it looks like," I quipped back. Wasting no time at all, I licked my lips and wrapped my right fist around his long, hard shaft. Precum leaked from his tip, and I swiped at the beads of pearly liquid with the pad of my thumb before locking eyes with him and parting my lips for a taste.

"Fuck, Zinn." His groan filled the air, and happiness swamped me. *Not yet but soon,* I mused in my head.

I hadn't let myself imagine anything like this for a long time. Camp continued to live in my head and heart rent-free for so long despite our contentious relationship. Nothing prepared me for returning home and coming face to face with him again. Our rivalry evaporated like some apparition after years apart, and now we were here.

Stroking his shaft, I held Camp's darkening gaze for a long moment until I couldn't hold back anymore.

My closed lips grazed across his crown before parting them and taking him into my mouth.

"Fuck!" He groaned again. *Fuck is right.* I moaned at the way he stuffed my mouth with only a few inches. "Baby..." Camp's hands made their way to my head, holding me there but not to force or hurry my actions. And that was a good thing because I had plans to tease him. I swiped and swirled my tongue around his crown and down the length of his cock, following the line of a pronounced vein. A temptation begging for some attention.

"Mm." I stroked him lazily, feeling the way his broad body twitched and trembled above me, his cock jerking in my mouth and grip. God, I loved this. Loved getting to have my wicked way with him like one of my many fantasies come to life.

"Zinn..." He uttered my name on the tail of another delicious rumble, and I redoubled my efforts, wanting to feel him come apart because of me. Unfortunately, the impatient man ruined all of my good intentions when he bent down and plucked me away from my evening snack and forced me to stand up.

"What the hell?!"

"What the hell is right, sweetheart. I was fixin' to blow."

Wearing a look on my face that I was pretty sure said 'And?!' his hands found their way to the panties I neglected to take off. In no time, he had me completely stripped, divested of the last remaining articles of clothing.

"I need to be inside you."

"You were already inside me," I reminded him, infusing a bratty tone into my voice that was only half serious.

His palms cupped my ass cheeks, squeezing them before lifting me up. My heart jumped as I squeaked at the surprise move.

"You know exactly what I mean, Zinn. I want your tight pussy pulsing around my cock until we both cum. Understand?"

"Mm." My body flushed anew with heat. "Let's do that then."

The wolfish grin that got my heart racing teased his lips for a good minute until I blinked. Then the next moment Camp pushed his way inside, unraveling me in the best way possible. Belatedly, I realized this time felt different somehow. More intense. Raw. Bare. And then it hit me all at once at the same time as Camp.

Bottoming out, his eyes widened with a look of pained horror mixed with the greatest pleasure.

"Zinn, I'm–"

"It's okay. I'm on birth control."

"Fuck, I wasn't thinking."

"Neither was I, but I'm okay. We're okay."

"We're more than okay, baby. You're mine. No matter what. Now and forever."

Done speaking with words, he continued with actions instead. His first thrust was slow but powerful, making me tingle from head to toe. Sandwiched between the wall and his body, Camp fucked me as if I belonged to him. Like I was his and his alone.

Wrapping my arms around his shoulders tightly, I completely melted into him. The sensations felt too monumental to do anything else. His stroke game had my body on edge quicker than expected, everything heightened between us even more tonight.

Inexplicable. Intense. My hips rolled uncontrollably at the contact. Meeting him thrust for thrust. Stroke for stroke until I was climbing to new heights. At the highest point of pleasure, the only thing I could do was crash. Splendidly.

I shattered, clenching around his pulsing shaft. The moment my orgasm slammed into me, I shuddered. And then Camp followed, his first shot of cum surprising a gasp right out of me. The sensation was so new and different.

"Fuck, Zinn." The intimate moment stretched and lingered like never before, rocking the both of us. Especially me. To my very core.

I couldn't help the way my limbs sort of loosened and relaxed into Camp; my body replete with a level of satisfaction and safety unknown to me before now.

I moaned and whimpered at the slightest movement Camp made, his half-hard cock slipping out of me slowly as our bodies cooled down. At the last second, he pushed his way back in, and I blinked heavy eyelids open to see him.

"Again?" I gasped.

His gaze had the same intense look that got us here in the first place. For a moment, I thought about what it would feel like to have him look at me this way for the rest of our lives.

As if he somehow heard my wishful thinking, Camp said, "Always."

Making sure his hold stayed secure, he hoisted me up and my arms wrapped around his shoulders again. Still connected in the most intimate way, he walked us to his bedroom where we made love again. Exactly like he promised.

Epilogue

I woke up slowly. Knowing it was the weekend, neither my body nor brain were in rush mode. I could languish in bed a little longer if I wanted to. But it seemed like my man had other ideas.

Hearing footsteps and the bedroom door opening, I forced myself to full wakefulness; curiosity getting the best of me. What caught my attention almost had me spreading my legs again in invitation even though I had no business doing that.

My body protested at the thought running through my head due to the delicious aches and pangs I knew would linger for a while today.

"Perfect. You're up."

"What's this?" I shimmied underneath the covers for a hot minute, taking in the scene that could only be described as a dream. *Maybe I'm still asleep after all.* The thought brought a smile to my face.

"Breakfast in bed," Camp said, and my smile grew bigger.

"And where did you find this?" I asked, referring to the large food tray he had loaded with small plates and a glass of juice. It wasn't something I'd noticed lying around the house at all.

"I got it just for this type of occasion."

"You're gonna spoil me rotten."

"Yep." His response held no hesitation or remorse.

This man. I wanted to roll my eyes but didn't because I low-key loved every bit of his attention and care. I sat up in bed and lifted my head, trying to see all the goodies he prepared on the tray. Camp was a prince among men; that's all I had to say. My lips smacked together anticipating the unexpected morning surprise.

He chuckled while gingerly placing the tray over my lap. My eyes widened at the eggs, bacon, and waffles on the plate. Too much for me to eat alone. Between the two of us, though, nothing would go to waste.

As I reached for a fork, something out of place stole my attention. My heart rate picked up speed at the same time my mouth went dry.

My right hand bypassed the fork and the promise of a delicious meal, itching to know about the random item in the left corner of the tray. An item that reminded me suspiciously of a jewelry box.

"Camp, what's this?" I felt like a parrot, repeating the same question again and again.

"How about you see for yourself, baby?"

My heart thumped behind my ribcage loud enough that I figured Camp could hear it. I was on edge with nerves. My hand shook at the first touch to the velvety surface. Soft. Expensive. Those were the only words my brain could come up with.

"Open it, Zinnia." At a loss to do anything else, I followed his order, picking up the small, velvet box and bringing it closer to me.

Taking deep breaths, I gathered my composure as much as possible. I forced my eyelids open after they fluttered closed and brought my free hand in on the action, stretching this moment out for all it was worth. Just in case I had it all wrong or something. Out of the corner of my eye, I registered movement, but nothing could wrench my focus away from the box in my grasp.

Finally, I exerted enough force to open the box with my heart on my sleeve even though it couldn't be what I wanted it to be. Not this soon.

All the air swooshed out of my lungs when light came from the half-open box. Tears gathered. The sight before me was unreal. What dreams were made of. And yet, I tried to blink the image away for a second. I couldn't let my hopes get out of hand.

"Zinn, look at me."

Unbeknownst to me, the breakfast tray had been moved. And Camp was eye-level with me now. On his knees next to the mattress. Scratch that. On closer inspection, he was on one-bended knee. My tears flowed faster than a waterfall.

"You might think this is next level crazy on my part, but I'm serious. More serious than I've ever been in my life. I've been in love with you since high school. You are my sister's best friend. My verbal sparring partner. And the one woman who's always captured my attention. I plan to love, protect, honor, and cherish you for the rest of our lives. Will you marry me, Zinn? I promise to make you so happy, baby."

"Yes, yes, yes. You already do."

He slipped the beautiful diamond on my ring finger, and I lunged for him then. Thankfully, he had the forethought to move the tray or else our breakfast would've been a casualty. Nothing else mattered at this moment but him. Me and him. Our lips clashed in an emotional, messy kiss that had me falling deeper in love with him. Madly. Unequivocally.

There was no getting around it. Or hiding the truth. My teenage crush had grown wings.

Camp climbed up on the bed, joining me. His kiss took my breath away. Lightheaded as if I floated above the clouds.

"What about–" He pulled away only to snatch off the T-shirt and shorts he'd put on to make our meal.

"Breakfast can wait," he grumbled, like he'd become an expert at reading my mind. After all this time knowing him, maybe he had. "I need you. Now and always."

"Well, pluck me sideways." I smiled at the momentary confusion crossing his handsome face. Grabbing his shoulders, I pulled him down on me and landed the juiciest kiss on my man. My fiancé.

This all felt like a dream, but it wasn't. This time with Camp was just what dreams were made of. And we'd have plenty more of them. A lifetime in fact.

Bloom where you are planted.

The saying that had frustrated me all those months ago circled back around in my mind. Although California would forever have a place in my heart, it wasn't where I was meant to be. That realization hit me like a ginormous flowerpot over the head.

My roots had always been here in Dallas. My hometown. Closest to my friends and family. And right here with the guy who still loved to rile me up. But this time, it was only in the best ways possible.

The End

Follow Me

Also by Kelly Violet

The Reawakening Series

Touch Me Softly, Book 1
Find Me Lonely, Book 2
Heal Me Gently, Book 3
Strongest With You, Book 4

All The Ways Duo

All The Pleasure
All The Passion

Suited for Love

Masked Up

Suited Up

Standalones

The Names You Call Me
The Love You Give Me
Hallowed Crush

About the Author

Kelly Violet is a born-and-raised New Yorker, living in a California world. A voracious romance reader, she published her first novel, Touch Me Softly, in December 2017. You can expect her stories to be angsty and gut-wrenching, fun and flirty, or just downright naughty. Music and dancing are her go-to outlets. If there's a party and dance floor (optional), rest assured that she will be one of the first people to bust a move.

Kelly loves to hear from readers. Connect with her on her various social media sites.